RICK BRANT'S **SCIENCE
PROJECTS**

The RICK BRANT SCIENCE-ADVENTURE *Stories*

BY JOHN BLAINE

———•••———

RICK BRANT'S
SCIENCE PROJECTS

BY JOHN BLAINE

APPLEWOOD BOOKS
Bedford, Massachusetts

To the Modern Reader:
Rick Brant's Science Projects was originally published in 1960. This facsimile reproduction is being made available as a service to those who remember the Rick Brant series fondly. It is not intended to be used as an actual book of science projects, nor have the projects contained herein been tested to meet today's requirements. Anyone attempting to carry out any of the projects within this book does so at his or her own risk, and neither the publisher, AmericanWebBooks, its parent, Applewood Books, Inc., Spindrift Island Publishing, the estate of Harold L. Goodwin, nor the John Blaine/Rick Brant Trust assume any liability for such use of this book.

Thank you for purchasing an Applewood book. Applewood reprints America's lively classics—books from the past that are still of interest to modern readers. For a free copy of our current catalog, write to:

Applewood Books
P.O. Box 365
Bedford, MA 01730

ISBN: 1-55709-008-4

10 9 8 7 6 5 4 3 2 1

Preface

THE IDEA for a science projects book to augment the Rick Brant series seems to have surfaced first sometime around the Summer of 1955. At that time, my father, Harold L. Goodwin (AKA John Blaine) wrote his publisher, Anne Hagen, at Grosset and Dunlap, Inc. (G&D) and suggested that:

> It occurs to me that there is another field... using the series for a springboard. I'm talking about... the young hunger for facts, especially about—but not limited to—the sciences. In brief, it is possible that a small, thin book series—really hard cover pamphlets—might be designed.... These books would be devoted to science, or factual explanations of things in the series books. For instance, out of my own series: The Rick Brant Book of Secret Codes and Ciphers, The Rick Brant Book of Sport Diving, The Rick Brant Book of Scientific Experiments, The Rick Brant Amateur Radio Handbook, The Rick Brant Book of Light Plane Flying, The Rick Brant Book of Electronic Brains. Each designed to give the young readers useful facts on the subject. Codes and ciphers he can use, and which his friends can't break. Advice on sport diving and equipment, how to use it, and

where. Scientific experiments he can do himself at
home. The basics of amateur radio. Types of light
planes, flying clubs, cost of instruction, careers in
flying. Electronic control experiments a junior
high school boy can perform, including the building of a miniature brain, and of an electronic
"creature" that works.

Dad opined that he could "do three or even four
books of the length suggested (5000–8000 words of
text) in a matter of weeks, since I have the subject matter cold from previous research." He provided a proposal for a new series of fact books based on the Rick
Brant books, and observed "Rick Brant sales are
approaching the half million mark; as of June 30,
1955, sales had passed 408,000." He noted that single
book sales indicated a minimum of 90,000 Rick Brant
fans. Dad's involvement with strategic planning for
science education is clear in the proposal, as well. He
wrote, fully two years before Sputnik, "The time is
right. During the next few years, there will be intensive
campaigns to interest more young people in science
and technology. Interest created by these campaigns,
which are being designed to overcome the shortage of
technicians and scientists, will carry over into young
reading habits. Boys and girls who read Rick Brant are
already interested in science...." The biography provided with the proposal to Grosset and Dunlap, Inc.
noted that "For the past few years, John Blaine has
been engaged in research on nuclear weapons, and has
participated in atomic test series in Nevada and the
Pacific.... His hobbies are much like those of Rick

Brant. Mr. Blaine is a qualified skin and Scuba diver, photographer, field archer and bow hunter, light plane pilot, and sling expert." At the time, Dad was Director, Atomic Test Operations, Federal Civil Defense Administration (FCDA), an agency to which he was "activated" from the National Security Resources Board (NSRB) in 1951.

Discussions with Grosset and Dunlap, Inc. evolved until March, 1956, when Dad received a letter from none other than the famed William Morris, at that time Editor-in-Chief at G&D. Morris suggested a single volume format "approximately twice the bulk of the present Rick Brant books, to retail at $1.95 and to be sold through the same outlets as our series books...." That letter contained a postscript that reads: "Since dictating this letter, the contract has been drawn and I am sending it along to you. Why not look it over and we can discuss any points that need clarification when you come in to the office."

In February, 1958, Dad left his position with FCDA to become Science Advisor to the Director, United States Information Agency. That month, he again wrote his editor, Anne Hagen, to let her know that G&D would have the manuscript for the *Pirates of Shan* "by the middle of next month," and he went on to note "I'm already at work on the Rick Brant Do-It-Yourself-if-you-dare book. I still haven't a really good salable title." He offered, "If Bill Morris approves, I'd like to send a detailed outline, then follow it with a personal visit to discuss... the art work, point of view, and so on." Norman Hoss, Managing Editor at G&D, responded, "Your plan... sounds fine."

Follow-up correspondence shortly thereafter posed the question to G&D: "Do we play Rick up as the putative author, or is this to be a 'John Blaine' production? I rather favor the latter, with ample mention of Rick but without personalizing him." Dad offered, "I'll whomp up a list of titles to accompany the outline so you can have a basis for choosing or dreaming up something else." The postscript to that February, 1958 letter noted "I'm returning the copies of the old contract for any necessary revision. I believe I can get copy to you by May 1st."

In March of that year, Regina Wirth, Secretary to Norman Hoss, Managing Editor at G&D, forwarded a revised contract for Rick Brant's Science Mysteries. The whopping first draw was $500 to the author.

Delays in writing the book must have ensued, at least in some measure due to pressure for another series book from G&D. In October, 1958, Norman Hoss wrote about the fact book: "Don't let this job interfere with the Rick Brant fiction titles, since continuation of the series is by far the most important assignment."

The next correspondence on the Science Projects book dates from January, 1959. At that time, Norman Hoss wrote "I am delighted with the first chapter of the Rick Brant fact book. The subject matter is interesting, the coverage is good, and the tone of writing is just right. So push ahead! I hope the rest of the book comes easier."

The correspondence files indicate that at least part of the reason for delay was continuing pressure from G&D to produce the next Rick Brant series book: an

April 1st letter that year pertaining to the *Blue Ghost Mystery* noted that the artwork for that volume needed to be started in six weeks. It urged that "the manuscript should be ready for release to the printer before the start of the summer vacation season." Within the week, Dad responded: "It isn't possible to finish both the fact book and the BGM before the start of the summer vacation season, unless said vacation starts in late August."

This letter provides insight to the writing process, and its empirical basis, as well. Dad wrote: "I've had trouble with my radio circuits, and had to take time out to build a couple of radios. As of now, it seems most likely that the fact book would not be finished until about May 10th." He closed by noting, "On present schedule, the Fact Book by mid-May, BGM by late August. Or, BGM by July 1, Fact Book by September 1st. You (Anne Hagen), Norm (Hoss), and Bill (Morris) will have to decide, and let me know."

Exactly when the manuscript was submitted is unclear, but the galleys were returned to Dad on February 26, 1960, along with a letter providing detail on book length and layout. Norman Hoss wrote: "Ted's (Tedesco, Art Director at G&D) count shows 228 pages of text without illustrations or front matter.... If we get the front matter into six pages, this leaves 22 pages for illustrations. We can't tell you exactly how much to cut until we dummy up the book with the illustrations in place.... The trim size of the page is 5 3/8" X 8" and there are 39 lines of type on a full page. We can run illustrations into the margins, but we should keep them at least 1 inch from the edges." The subsequent cover letter accompanying the page proofs was not dated, but Norman Hoss, Managing Editor at G&D, asked for "as quick a turnaround as possible." The rush was on, because Hoss wrote: "We don't usually send out the reader's set, figuring on transferring the author's corrections to it before the printer gets it. But in the interests of time and because you're an old pro, I thought I'd ask you to mark it for the printer. If there are any queries to me or Ted (Tedesco), write them on a separate slip and slip them in the proof."

Dad ultimately returned the page proofs on June 7, 1960, with relatively minor edits. He stated that the book "looks fine." His biggest concern seems to have been that some of the illustrations were designed to fit sideways on the page, and he suggested that "Ted can correct those that run into the gutters."

Dad's government personnel records, in particular his SF 86, "Security Investigative Data for Sensitive Position," indicate that during the period Science Projects was in the works, and specifically between 1958 and 1960, he traveled, "on official business to Egypt, India, Sweden, Denmark, France, Germany, Austria, Switzerland, Italy, England, New Zealand, and Antarctica." I still have the Christmas Card he sent from Operation Deep Freeze, South Pole Station, in 1960. But on the home front, Dad also found time to be the Den Leader for my Cub Scout Den, trying out and teaching some of the lessons that made it into the Science Projects book. Den 8 scouts became novice field archers, we built radios from household supplies, we learned the sling, and we even practiced throwing tomahawks (Dad was a left-handed ace with the tomahawk and throwing knives). A number of those scouts went on to careers in science and technology, and all of them learned to appreciate hands-on adventures both outdoors and in the workshop.

It is hard to know what impact the Science Projects book had on young lives and future career decisions at a time when our nation was beginning to emphasize science education as a matter of national need and policy. Its author helped to shape that policy, and his commitment to science education continued to shape his own career, and his writings, throughout the remainder of his life. It is our hope that by reprinting *Rick Brant's Science Projects*, the original fans of the Rick Brant books will be able to rediscover the magic of their childhood as junior scientists and to pass on that love for science and adventure to their children and grandchildren.

For the family of John Blaine, and for his grandchildren (dba Spindrift Island Publishing), we hope you enjoy this first Rick Brant reprint.

—Dr. R. Christopher Goodwin
Comus, Maryland

Introduction

THIS BOOK was written because readers of the Rick Brant Science Adventures asked for it. A few letters to the author suggested a book, but most of them simply asked for details on how Rick and Scotty performed some of their experiments, or how they made slings, or how to use a book code.

Answering the letters individually with diagrams and construction details was not possible, but an answer in the form of a how-to-do-it book was. This book, then, is the result of letters from Rick's fans to the author.

All science and adventure projects mentioned in the Rick Brant books are covered, except for a few on which no letters or only one or two were received. A few additional projects are included for good measure, because the author knows from his experience that they are popular with boys.

Since Rick Brant is able to use adult laboratory equipment and has the help of a whole staff of scientists, he is naturally able to do many things beyond the reach of the average reader. But none of the projects in this book require either expert help or special equipment. Cost of materials has been kept low. Any boy with a paper route or some other source of a small income could do all of them. Boys with no income at all can do most of them.

One helpful tool in using this book will be a dictionary. Now and then the author has included a particularly good word that you may not know, and this was done deliberately as a kind of extra, easy research project. You can understand everything without a dictionary by skipping unfamiliar words, but it adds to the fun if you use one.

Some words can't be found in any dictionary because they are made-up words that sound like real ones but don't actually exist. Read about them in Chapter I. Try making up some yourself.

The main idea in using this book is to have fun.

A famous scientist once said that the only people who have the privilege of doing what they want to do most and getting paid for it at the same time are physicists and baseball players. He was right, but he didn't go quite far enough. He should have said scientists, professional athletes and explorers.

It is for those boys who enjoy the fun of science and adventure that this book was written.

JOHN BLAINE

Spindrift, 1960

Contents

Contents

Chapter I

How to Keep a Secret

> Rick looked closely at the number-covered sheet. "I don't know beans about codes," he said. "How can we decipher this thing?"
>
> "Your father has a large library," Scotty answered. "Would he have a book on cryptography?"
>
> from THE ROCKET'S SHADOW
> Chapter X, *A Message in Code.*

A SECRET, Rick Brant once said, is something only one person knows and never tells anyone else. If the person swears a friend to secrecy and passes on the secret, it is only a matter of time until the friend also swears a friend to secrecy—and so on. This continues until the secret is an "open secret," which means that everyone knows it, but it is only discussed in whispers.

This may be unfortunate, but it's also natural. Half the fun in knowing something interesting is to be able to tell a friend. The whole idea of cryptography, which is the name given to the science of secret writing, is to enable people to share secrets with friends while protecting the secrets from others.

Not many of us have secrets that must be hidden at all costs from a deadly and determined enemy. But even though lives do not hang on our secrets, and governments may not fall if they are revealed, we do have business that is our own and which we wish to keep private.

There is no need whatever to keep secrets from our families, but there are times when plans for a surprise party, for a surprise gift, or other similar activity should be protected. And if we want to be entirely candid, we'd better admit that we can help little (or big) brother and/or little (or big) sister to mind his/her business more effectively if we guard our affairs with the help of a little cryptography.

Quite apart from all this, it's just plain fun to be able to communicate with friends, fellow scouts, or club members in a good code or cipher, even if there are no secrets that need protection.

The ways of forming good codes and ciphers are based on easily understood principles, whether the purpose is to conceal plans for a surprise party or the mechanism of a ballistic missile.

To begin with, there are terms that should be understood for ease of operation and discussion. These are the principal ones:

Code   A code is not the same as a cipher. A code is a series of words, symbols, pictures, colors or sounds, each of which has an agreed meaning, and always has that meaning. A traffic light is a simple color code. More complicated codes require a code dictionary, or code book.

Cipher   A cipher is a means of sending an entire message, letter for letter. No dictionary or code book is needed. A cipher can be used with only a pencil and paper.

Clear   The original message, in plain English, is the clear.

Encipher/Decipher. To encipher is to put the clear into a cipher. To decipher is to translate a cipher into the clear again. **Encode and Decode** have the same meaning where codes are concerned.

Group A cipher is broken into groups for ease in transmission, and to help conceal the message. The standard number of letters or symbols in a group is five, because experience has shown that transmission over radio or wires is simplest and produces less error with this number. But any number can be used in a group, so long as all groups in the message have the same number.

Null A null is a letter or symbol put in to complete a message that doesn't come out even, or to complete a group, or to confuse.

With these terms established, we can get down to the business of devising ways to conceal messages.

First, we can reject codes. They have their place in some activities, but since they require a book, they are not best suited for common use. The Navy uses codes because a ship maneuver of a standard kind can be described with a single word or group of letters. Furthermore, the code book aboard ship is in no great danger of capture by an enemy. If capture is imminent, the code book can be thrown overboard. Navy codes are bound in lead to insure instant sinking.

There is one kind of code worthy of passing mention, because it uses a book already in existence. This kind is called a BOOK CODE, or DICTIONARY CODE.

In THE CAVES OF FEAR, Chahda, Indian friend

of the Spindrift gang, sends a message in a book code and uses the *World Almanac*, 1950 edition. The method described applies to all such codes. The first numbers in a group give the page, the remaining numbers give the line on the page and position of the word on the line. If a dictionary is used, the first numbers give the page and the second numbers give the word.

This kind of code is slow. Furthermore, if the "enemy" can guess the book, the entire code is automatically compromised, as the military experts say. Chahda had definite reasons for using such a code in the CAVES OF FEAR. The principal one was that he had never discussed codes and ciphers with Rick or Scotty; there was no agreed method of sending secret messages. Chahda had to figure out a way of sending a coded message that the Brants could understand but would be reasonably safe from anyone else.

Since ciphers need only a pencil and paper, they are by far the most practical for general use.

The learned monk of the middle ages, Sir Francis Bacon, has left us a form of cipher, but more than that, he has left us a guide for describing a good cipher. He said that the virtues of perfect ciphers should be . . .

that they be not laborious to write and read; that they be impossible to decipher; and, in some cases, that they be without suspicion.

This is a tall order. The first part will give us no difficulty. The second is probably impossible. The only cipher that we know of today that has never been broken is one that Francis Bacon himself devised. He wrote a book in this cipher. In spite of years of work by experts, it has never been read.

The third requirement, that the message be "without suspicion" is a little less difficult. A cipher can be made to look like an arithmetic paper, for example. It can be disguised as a penmanship exercise. There are many possibilities if concealment of the existence of a cipher is necessary.

To devise a useful cipher, we must first set up a standard. How secure must it be? We will assume that your message is unlikely to fall into the hands of an expert in cryptanalysis, in other words an expert at deciphering other peoples' codes and ciphers. But we will assume that your message has a reasonable chance of falling into the hands of someone who knows the elements of cryptography, perhaps from solving the newspaper cryptographic puzzles. You will know best about the degree of security needed. If low, pick the simplest kind of cipher. If high, pick one that's a bit more complicated.

Keep in mind that even an expert needs material on which to work. A single short message might be safe even from an expert. Several short messages would not be. This is because the expert depends on the frequency with which letters and combinations of letters appear. Unless he has enough material, he cannot be sure that the statistics he uses will apply to the message in hand. But more of this presently.

First, we must make a distinction between two

kinds of cipher: *Substitution* and *Transposition*. Either can be used, or they can be used in combination.

The most common form of substitution cipher is the Morse Code. The name is misleading, because it isn't a code at all, from the cryptographer's viewpoint. Each combination of dots and dashes stands for a single letter or number. The message is sent by substituting the proper combination of dots and dashes for each letter of the clear. Of course there is nothing secret about the Morse Code; it is a public cipher.

One of the earliest substitution ciphers came to us from Julius Caesar. Old Julius concealed his messages by substituting other letters of the alphabet according to a regular plan. That is, he counted three letters down the alphabet, taking D for A, E for B, F for C, and so on. By this method, RICK BRANT would become ULFN EUDQW.

The amount of security in such a system is very low. But if it should be enough, the system can most easily be applied through the use of a cipher wheel. Such a wheel is shown on page 17. One can be made from thin cardboard, with the two wheels held together by a paper fastener. Note that the movable alphabet in the illustrated wheel is backwards. This gives a slightly greater degree of security, but not enough for real safety.

Another very old example of simple substitution is the famous pigpen. It was used by freemasons long before the Renaissance and is still seen occasionally today, usually in schoolrooms. It has little security, however.

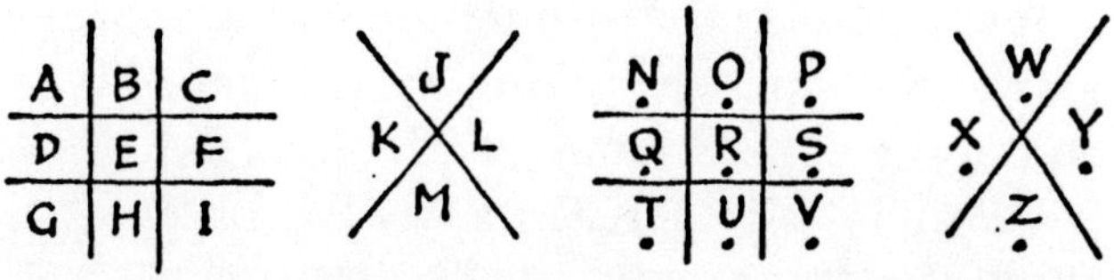

The name SPINDRIFT ISLAND, enciphered by pigpen, would look like this:

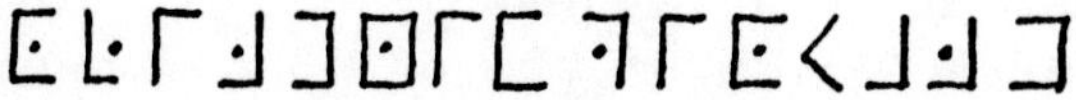

Security could be somewhat improved by using the pigpen with the cipher wheel. The message would first be enciphered by the wheel, then the enciphered text would be further enciphered by pigpen. But our advice is: don't bother. There are better ways.

If we substitute numbers for letters in a different way, we begin to develop a method that has better security, and is still easy to use. The simplest form would be to give each letter of the alphabet a number, but this is too simple.

We start our concealment with a single-alphabet cipher in a five by five block. Since there are 26 letters in the alphabet we must eliminate one. J is the usual one to drop, with I being used for both itself and J. We number the rows and columns of the block.

	1	2	3	4	5
1	A	B	C	D	E
2	F	G	H	I	K
3	L	M	N	O	P
4	Q	R	S	T	U
5	V	W	X	Y	Z

If our letter is G, we enter the second row, then look at the number heading the column. G is Second row, second column, or 22. Similarly, L is 31, S is 43 and Z is 55. RICK BRANT is 42–24–13–25 12–42–11–33–44.

But this is only a beginning. Many people know that letters of the alphabet occur with different frequencies, and that these frequencies are well known. For example, E is used far more frequently than any other letter. In English, it will appear 591 times in each thousand words, and 131 times in each thousand letters.

The order of frequencies with which letters appear is this: E T A O N R I S H D L F C M U G Y P W B V K X J Q Z.

Knowing this, a message can be broken down into the frequency of occurrence of each character, whether a number, a pigpen symbol, or a letter. This is elementary cryptanalysis. We can only avoid it by what is called *suppression of frequencies.*

The next step, then, is to create a different kind of block, nine by three, as follows:

	1	2	3	4	5	6	7	8	9
1, 4, 7	A	B	C	D	E	F	G	H	I
2, 5, 8	J	K	L	M	N	O	P	Q	R
3, 6, 9	S	T	U	V	W	X	Y	Z	

With this block we have a choice of combinations for each letter. E can be represented by 15, 45, or 75, and so on. Frequencies are effectively hidden by mixing up the combinations.

This is a pretty good cipher, for most purposes. If the message is short, even the trained specialist will have trouble solving it. The empty cell, which can be represented by 39, 69 or 99 makes an effective null and can even be used for punctuation. The cipher can also be varied by changing the numbers, so long as they are changed in an easily remembered pattern. We must always keep in mind Bacon's rule that ciphers "be not laborious to write and read."

There is one more step in substitution ciphers that will add to security, and that is the use of a key. The title of the third Rick Brant adventure, SEA GOLD, fits the requirement of a key—that no letter appear more than once in the key word or phrase. To use this key in our nine by three pattern, we set it up this way:

	1	2	3	4	5	6	7	8	9
1, 4, 7	S	E	A	G	O	L	D	B	C
2, 5, 8	F	H	I	J	K	M	N	P	Q
3, 6, 9	R	T	U	V	W	X	Y	Z	

Note that letters not included in the key simply follow in alphabetical order. Use of the key has the advantage that the alphabet is not in neat order and the cipher cannot be solved by guessing.

Using this cipher, let's encipher the message, BEWARE THE PIRATES OF SHAN. We find the number for each letter by entering the pattern on the horizontal line. B is 18, and so on.

18–42–35–43–91–72   32–22–12   88–53–
31–73–92–12–41   75–21   11–82–13–27.

In groups of five, our message reads:

18423   54391   72322   21288
53317   39212   41752   11182
13270

When the message is transcribed, it will be seen at once that the final 0 is a null. The receiver, knowing the pattern and the key word, should be able to decipher in a few minutes, jotting the pattern down for a reference.

It would take a whole book to cover the endless variations and elaborations of the substitution cipher. Things get more complicated from this point, too complicated for our simple objective of giving reasonable protection to the message.

Time now to consider the transposition cipher.

No new letters or symbols are used in the transposition cipher. The letters of the clear are scrambled according to a definite pattern, with confusing results. In its simplest form, the transposition may mean simply writing the message backwards, tub siht si oot elpmis. Instead, try this one:

TEHA   ETBS   RPAI
NNTD   SRLI   IFVT

This is an example of a very elementary cipher. To decipher, we break the groups of letters into pairs, reading from left to right, and list the pairs vertically.

T E
H A
E T
B S
R P
A I
N N
T D
S R
L I
I F
V T

By reading down the first column and then the second, we discover that THE BRANTS LIVE AT SPINDRIFT.

We could arrive at exactly the same cipher by setting up the message horizontally and taking the vertical pairs.

T H E B R A N T S L I V
E A T S P I N D R I F T

The most important thing in a transposition cipher is to agree on the method, and on the number of letters in a group.

For ease of use, the first step in the method is to select a pattern. In some of the fancier ciphers, triangles and odd shapes are used, but the standard is the rectangle. And among rectangles, we start with one that will contain an alphabet.

The reason for this choice is simplicity of illustration. But the four-by-six rectangle has definite advantages. It is easy to remember, it is big enough to contain most simple messages, and it offers just about as much variety as the larger patterns. This will be clear as we set down examples.

Since a four-by-six rectangle will contain only 24 letters, we eliminate J and V. I and W will serve for themselves and the missing letters.

Note the variety of ways in which the alphabet can be inserted into the pattern. This is important, because the message can be inserted the same way.

1.   HORIZONTAL

a.	b.
A B C D E F	F E D C B A
G H I K L M	M L K I H G
N O P Q R S	S R Q P O N
T U W X Y Z	Z Y X W U T

c.	d.
T U W X Y Z	Z Y X W U T
N O P Q R S	S R Q P O N
G H I K L M	M L K I H G
A B C D E F	F E D C B A

2.   VERTICAL

a.	b.
A E I N R W	W R N I E A
B F K O S X	X S O K F B
C G L P T Y	Y T P L G C
D H M Q U Z	Z U Q M H D

c.	d.
D H M Q U Z	Z U Q M H D
C G L P T Y	Y T P L G C
B F K O S X	X S O K F B
A E I N R W	W R N I E A

Note that the alphabet can start at any corner of the rectangle and go either horizontally or vertically. In the same way, it can start at any corner and then alternate lines:

```
A B C D E F
M L K I  H G
N O P Q R S
Z Y X W U T
```

Fancier versions include both diagonals and spirals. The diagonals are apt to be complicated, but the spirals are pretty easy. They can start at any corner.

```
I  H G F E D
K WUTS C
L  X Y Z R B
MN O P Q A
```

It is clear that the step to be taken after deciding on the pattern is how the message is to be written into the pattern. Any one of those suggested above can be chosen.

Once the message is in the pattern, it must be transcribed into the final cipher. Any route can be followed.

The final step is to agree on the number of letters in a group. Six or four will always come out even in this block, but five can be used by adding nulls.

Now, let's see how it works out in practice.

We agree to use the four by six block, which means four vertical and six horizontal rows.

We agree to insert the message by a horizontal route, starting in the upper right hand corner, like illustration 1.b.

We agree to transcribe the message into cipher by a vertical route, starting in the lower left-hand corner, as in illustration 2.c.

We agree on groups of five.

Now for a message. We wish to send: MEET ME AFTER SCHOOL AT THE OLD BARN. BRING SCOTTY. SIGNED JOE.

Here's a problem. Too many letters. The block
will only take 24. But we see that much can be
eliminated without changing the meaning. We
don't need to say "at the." We probably don't
need to say "me." The signature can be a simple J.

The message is still too long, so the next step is
to eliminate vowels. If "old" is needed for clear
identification, it should stay as is, but the rest of
the vowels can go, particularly if we've been using
the cipher for a while and all hands are used to the
standard abbreviations, like MT for meet and
SCL for school.

When we've finished chopping, we find exactly
24 letters in our message, which reads:

MT   FTR   SCL   OLD   BRN   BRNG
SCTTY   J

We insert the message in the block, as agreed:

S R T F T M
B D L O L C
G N R B N R
J Y T T C S

This is pretty thoroughly garbled as is, but we
proceed to transcribe the message into groups of
five, starting in the lower left-hand corner and
moving vertically:

JGBSY   NDRTR   LTTBO
FCNLT   SRCMI

We now have a message enciphered in a way
that will give excellent security. Elimination of the
vowels has thoroughly upset the frequency tables,

and the rest is so much alphabet hash to the casual viewer. Note that we used the J, although it was eliminated from the alphabet. In a substitution cipher the J would have remained out. But in this case it makes no difference. The alphabets were only for illustration.

To decipher, of course, the receiver works the message backwards. He puts the message down on his work sheet, starting in the lower left-hand corner and working up. When completed, he writes the message in normal order, taking it a letter at a time from the horizontal route, starting in the upper right hand corner. He deciphers perfectly.

Fortunes of war enter at this point. The Teacher catches him at it, by asking him a question while he's concentrating. He has to stay after school. The rendezvous is never completed. But anyway, the cipher worked perfectly.

The next step in achieving security—if the ciphers given are not enough—is to do a double encipherment. First put the message into a transposition cipher, then put the enciphered message into a substitution cipher. This should stand up under even expert scrutiny, if the message is short. Remember that the experts can crack most codes and ciphers but they need plenty of material in the code or cipher to do it.

A combination of code and cipher is sometimes simple and useful. Individuals can be given code names, so can places. If the old barn is a regular hangout call it something for code purposes, preferably short. If Scotty is a regular member of the group, give him a code designation for message purposes. Let the message read:

MT   FTR   SCL   OX   BRNG   SY.

It is also possible to devise verbal codes. Such a code could be as extensive as a new language, but this is pretty hard work, and probably not necessary. Doubletalk is useful, because the words sound as though you were saying something, but are actually gibberish. Give such words code meanings. Then when you murmur, "Dilp the prodsponder under the spanson," it won't matter if you're overheard, because only the fellow tribesman at the next desk will know you're warning him to hide the comic book under the lesson paper.

If you want to be really elaborate about a verbal code, learn a little bit of some unusual foreign tongue. This isn't too hard unless you settle down to really learn it. Just pick out the phrases you need, but make no attempt to pronounce them properly. In fact, give them a regional American accent.

Enough phrases for most use can be found in the little language handbooks put out by the Armed Services for the use of servicemen in foreign lands. There's one in Tagalog. Others are in Arabic, Hindi, Persian and most European languages. The Superintendent of Documents, Washington, D. C., can send you a list, and sell them to you. They're very inexpensive. Write for Price List 19.

The history of the world is filled with tales of codes and ciphers, of all kinds. There isn't room in a single chapter to treat the complexities of secret writing, much less the tales of adventure that go with cryptographic history. But these tales have been told elsewhere, one of the most interesting sources being Fletcher Pratt's *Secret and Urgent*. For further study, Laurence Dwight Smith's *Cryptography* will also prove useful.

But for now:

KPEHE   EPRYS   OIUMR   PCLIE
TE   HN   ED

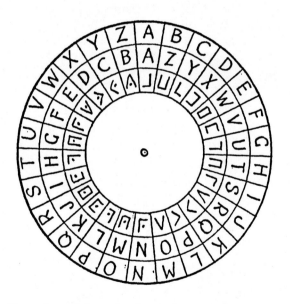

To make a cipher wheel, put the outer letters on one piece of cardboard and the inner letters and symbols on another and fasten them together at the center.

Chapter II

Ancient Weapon for Modern Sportsmen

Scotty placed the stone in the pouch and gripped it in his left hand, holding the stone in place with thumb and forefinger. He took throwing position . . . released the pouch and put his solid weight into the throw.

Rick's lips pursed in a silent whistle. The stone sang shrilly as it flew up, up, up, and far out. Then the trajectory dropped off rapidly and it fell into the sea. "Bless Bess!" Rick exclaimed. "Three hundred yards if it was an inch!"

from THE SCARLET LAKE MYSTERY
Chapter I, *Spindrift.*

IN THE SCARLET LAKE MYSTERY, Rick Brant and his pal Scotty make good use of slings. The word sling conjures up a mental picture in most people —a picture of a wooden fork with rubber bands and a leather pouch. Such gadgets were, and still are, common. When made, they use the fork of a tree branch with rubber bands cut from an old tire tube. If bought, the weapon is made of laminated wood with bands of surgical rubber tubing. But in either case it's a slingshot, not a sling.

The invention of the slingshot had to wait for the invention of the automobile, and an easy and free source of rubber for propulsion of stones. The sling, however, is older than recorded history. Since it could be made of animal hide, it needed no other invention than the genius of a human mind.

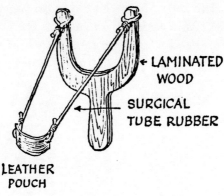

← LAMINATED WOOD

SURGICAL TUBE RUBBER

LEATHER POUCH

THIS IS A MODERN SLINGSHOT
NOT A SLING

But where using a slingshot is mostly a matter of having a good eye, the sling demands the same kind of coordination found in tennis, with body, hand and eye working together. There are few greater satisfactions in any sport than to put a sling stone where it is aimed, perhaps at a distance of a hundred yards or more.

The sling can be made in less than half a day, from materials found around the house. It tucks into the smallest pocket with room to spare. It uses the most plentiful of ammunition—stones. And, when properly made and used, it has great range.

It can also—and this is a warning—be deadly.

Witness this event, recorded in the Book of Samuel, in the Old Testament of the Bible.

. . . Then he [David] took his staff in his hand, and chose five smooth stones from the brook, and

put them in his shepherd's bag, in his wallet; his sling was in his hand, and he drew near to the Philistine.

. . . And David put his hand in his bag and took out a stone, and slung it, and struck the Philistine on his forehead; the stone sank into his forehead, and he fell on his face to the ground.

The Philistine, of course, was the giant Goliath, who may have been as much as eight feet tall. This is not incredible. There were Polynesian chieftains that tall.

In any case, the sling was known in pre-Biblical times. No one knows how old the weapon is. It was probably one of the earliest weapons invented, because it works on a principle man discovered when some early genius picked up a stick and banged someone with it. The principle is that of making the arm longer.

The spear, in a direct sense, is an extension of the arm when used for stabbing. But of greater importance is the length added to the spearman's arm by the throwing stick, the specially contrived holder with which the spear is thrown.

Not all early peoples developed the throwing stick. Those who did got greater range and velocity in their throws than those who didn't, because the longer the arm, the greater the ability to hurl a weapon.

A bat operates on the same principle. The circuit clout of the heavy hitter is performed with a full swing. With the bat choked up, no home run results, but a short and effective bunt can be laid down. This is no accident. The distance the ball travels is in direct proportion to the amount by which the bat lengthens the batter's arms.

The sling is also a flexible extension of a man's arm. In this case the man is throwing a stone, but the principle is the same. The sling is probably the cheapest and most effective arm-extender ever devised.

When you hold a sling, which is nothing but a length of cord and a cloth pouch, it's hard to imagine that you're holding a weapon of war. But you'd better imagine it, and develop a healthy respect for the thing. It has helped to make history.

The Assyrians were among the most famous of the early slingmen, and their monuments show us curly-bearded warriors with slings in hand or in use. The people of the Balearic Islands were another famous group of slingmen.

The Bible records warfare between the Tribe of Benjamin and the Children of Israel. Special mention is made of the Benjaminites' crack corps of left-handed slingmen who could "sling a stone at a hair and never miss."

The Roman Legions had their "Funditores," slingmen recruited mostly from Greece, Syria and Northern Africa.

Slingmen fought side by side with the armored Frankish knights, not only in Europe, but during the Crusades. Many and many an Arab Paladin (Have Sword, Will Scrap) was laid low by a sling-stone.

As a matter of history, the earliest artillery descended directly from the sling. These early field pieces heaved huge boulders. They were called catapults and trebuchets. Archimedes the Greek, the first artilleryman to win himself a big reputation as a quick-on-the-draw stoneslinger, probably got his ideas from the sling and the staff sling. This latter weapon was a kind of super sling, of which more later.

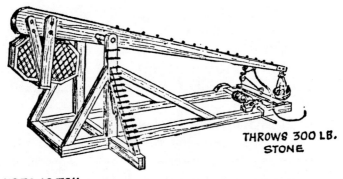

THROWS 300 LB. STONE

UP TO 10 TON WEIGHT

Eventually catapult and trebuchet gave way to cannon, while the hand sling gave way to the long bow and the crossbow.

In later years, many of the old weapons were revived, not for war but for sport. The English long bow and its cousins are still very much with us. The crossbow is back too, although most states forbid its use as a hunting weapon. The blowgun of Africa and the Americas has regained some interest among sportsmen, and the spear survives as the javelin in intercollegiate and Olympic sports. Even the Australian boomerang has its fans.

The sling, however, has practically vanished. Only a few sportsmen know how to use it. What makes this so surprising is that all other sports equipment either costs a fair amount or is time consuming to make, while the sling costs practically nothing and can be made in an hour or two.

This is not to say a sling can be used well and accurately by everyone, anymore than everyone can shoot a round of golf in par or bat .300. Like all sports, slinging is more art than science, and it takes practice—plenty of it.

To get down to cases: let's examine a sling.

If we look at an ancient one, we may see that it is cut from a single piece of leather, the cords widening out to form a pouch that is shaped while wet. Or, leather thongs may be fastened to a piece of suitable pouch leather.

The ancients used leather because it was the only strong material they had. But we're lucky in having a wide choice. We can make a sling with less effort.

This is what's needed:

The Pouch Readymade material for a pouch is heavy canvas. This canvas can be a piece of old tarpaulin, if it's still sound and whole. A pair of discarded sneakers is another possible source, if they will yield a single piece of strong material from the inside of the foot. These pieces from sneakers are already shaped by the ankle bone.

The size is about 3 x 4 inches, or perhaps a little larger. It's a matter of personal choice. A smaller piece would probably not be suitable for most boys.

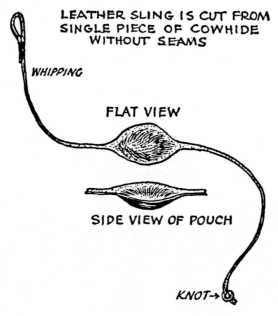

LEATHER SLING IS CUT FROM SINGLE PIECE OF COWHIDE WITHOUT SEAMS

WHIPPING

FLAT VIEW

SIDE VIEW OF POUCH

KNOT→

Sailcloth is a possibility for those who live near the water.

If none of these is at hand, you probably have a discarded pair of dungarees around the house.

Don't buy pouch material. Find something that will do.

The cloth should be closely woven and strong. It should be fairly stiff, like good canvas. If it isn't that stiff, use more than one layer. If you must use unbleached muslin, sugar or feed-sack cloth or an old rainhat, make it of multiple layers to get strength and some stiffness.

The Cord Strong, dependable cord is an absolute must. A cord that breaks at the wrong moment could do considerable damage to people or property by letting the stone go at the wrong time.

Cord used for wrapping packages is most easily found, but be careful. Most of it is not strong enough. Or, if it is strong, it may be hard to handle, because it kinks. If it's thick cotton cord, it may do.

In general, the best cords are woven rather than twisted. Chalk line is an exception.

Venetian blind cord would be good. Nylon venetian-blind cord would be much better.

Nylon, dacron and other synthetic fibers are made into a variety of cord sizes these days, and they're not hard to obtain.

The size of the cord is less important than strength and flexibility. It should be large enough so it won't cut your hand as thread can do. From $3/32$ to $1/8$ of an inch would be about right.

If you must buy cord, chalk line will serve very well. It is twisted instead of woven, but it is strong and inexpensive in a small ball.

As to length: let the cord hang from your hand to the ground. Double the length. Then add a separate piece a foot long.

The Thread Check with the family's expert seamstress. In houses where sewing is done—and that's most of them—the sewing kit is apt to contain a strong thread used for sewing on coat buttons. Any thread that will hold an overcoat button through a hard winter is plenty strong enough. If you have to buy thread, consult with the clerk at the variety store. Explain that you need something really tough.

No other materials are needed. The tools consist of a pair of scissors with which to cut the pouch to size, and some means of sewing.

Machine sewing is best. But with care, hand sewing can be about as strong—it just takes longer.

HERE'S HOW A SLING IS MADE

1. Make the pouch at least 3 x 4 inches or slightly larger, but keep the proportions. It should be longer than it is wide. If in doubt, find a stone about the size of a golf ball and try it in the pouch. It should be held with enough room, but without too much extra material on the sides. If the pouch wraps around the stone too loosely, add another layer. It should wrap around, but not whip enough to hold the stone from release.

THE POUCH

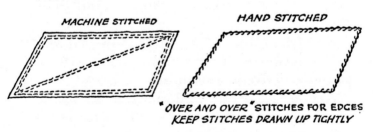

MACHINE STITCHED   HAND STITCHED

"OVER AND OVER" STITCHES FOR EDGES
KEEP STITCHES DRAWN UP TIGHTLY

2. Whether of a single layer or two or three, the pouch should be sewn. This is to keep it from unraveling at the edges. A double row of machine

stitches close to the edge would be fine. If you're doing it by hand, sew a series of loops around the edges.

3. If machine sewn, running stitches from corner to corner in an X pattern will add strength and stiffness.

4. The pouch is ready for the cord. Study the illustration. Notice that the long piece of cord goes along one side of the pouch while the short piece goes along the other. Of course both cords are centered, with equal lengths extending on both sides of the pouch. Hold the cords in place with a couple of hand stitches.

ATTACHING THE CORDS

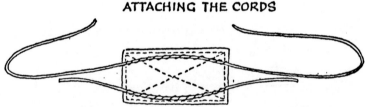

MAKE PATTERN OF CORD LAYOUT ON POUCH SYMMETRICAL. CORDS CURVE AS SHOWN BY UPPER CORD

5. The cords are located on the outside of the pouch. If you have a sewing machine working for you, run it back and forth across the cords until they are firmly stitched in place. If it's a hand job, bring the needle up from inside the pouch, across the cord and back down again, repeating over and over until the cord is sewn tightly to the pouch fabric. Go right through the cord in a few places. Then, if the stitches loosen, the cord won't slip.

6. Next step is to bring the cords together. Study the illustration. It is important to join the

cords on the center line of the pouch so it will be evenly balanced. If in doubt, lay the pouch on a long piece of paper. Find the center line and extend this line past the point where the cords will meet. Then make them meet on the line you've drawn.

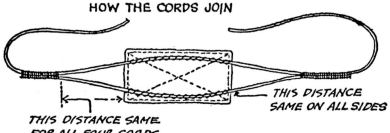

HOW THE CORDS JOIN

THIS DISTANCE SAME ON ALL SIDES

THIS DISTANCE SAME FOR ALL FOUR CORDS

7. Check the measurements as shown in the drawing. When you're satisfied that all is right, whip the strings together. Use thread, if heavy enough. Or, if it's hard to handle, most any good string will do including a length of fishline. Follow the illustration. Secure the ends with a needle, if you like. It will make the whipping even more secure.

8. Now the sling is done, except for final measurements. Hold both cords in your throwing hand. Put a stone in the pouch and let it hang. Adjust the cords until the pouch hangs evenly, with both cords of equal length. The bottom of the weighted pouch should be just above your shoe tops. Mark the cords where they emerge from your fingers. A dot of ink is best. In one cord make a loop just above the mark. The loop should be big enough for your index finger. Make it big enough for

comfort. In the other cord, just above the mark, tie a figure eight knot, sometimes called a blood knot. Slip the loop on your forefinger, take the knot between that fingertip and your thumb, and let the weighted pouch hang down again. If it hangs evenly, you've finished. If not, work on the loop and knot until it does. Then trim off the loose ends, leaving a quarter inch. That's it. You've made a sling.

Now for the open spaces. And make no mistake, you'll need plenty of space. While you're getting the hang of it stones will fly in all directions, including backwards. Don't trust your eagle eye to shoot down a street. You won't even be able to hit the city, at first.

WHIPPING THE CORDS

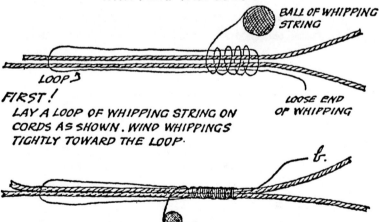

FIRST!

LAY A LOOP OF WHIPPING STRING ON CORDS AS SHOWN. WIND WHIPPINGS TIGHTLY TOWARD THE LOOP.

SECOND!

PASS THE WHIPPING (a) THROUGH THE LOOP, THEN PULL THE LOOSE END (b) UNTIL THE LOOP IS PULLED UNDER THE WRAPPINGS, TAKING THE END OF THE WHIPPING WITH IT. TRIM LOOSE ENDS

You'll also need ammunition. The story of David and Goliath doesn't mention it, but you can be sure David chose stones of the same weight and about the same size. Ideal ammunition would be identical, but this is impossible, so do the best you can. For a starter, match up stones in several sizes, shapes and weights, so you can see which is best for you. Standardize when you're an expert.

The reason for matching ammunition is that different shapes and weights of stones behave in different ways, naturally enough. You can't get the same results every time with unmatched ammo.

Comes now the hard part—learning to use the sling.

Consider the problem. The sling and stone are in front of you. What you want is for the stone to come down over your shoulder as though you were serving a tennis ball.

FIGURE 8 KNOT AND OVERHAND LOOP

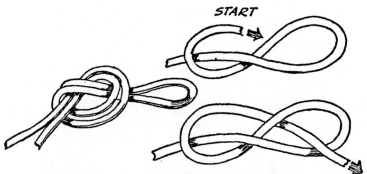

START

FINISH

DRAW UP TIGHT WHEN LOOP IS RIGHT SIZE
AND IN THE RIGHT PLACE. EXPERIMENT
UNTIL YOU GET IT RIGHT.

To do this, you must get the stone into position.

You start with loop on forefinger, knot held in thumb and forefinger. You stand facing at nearly right angles to your target. If you're a right-hander, your left shoulder is pointing a little to the left of the target. If you're a left-hander, your right shoulder is pointing a little to the right of the target.

Your throwing hand, with loop and knot held in place, is about at your belt buckle. The hand holding the pouch is extended comfortably, but higher than your throwing hand. This hand almost points at the target. The position should be comfortable, and you should be perfectly balanced. If you're not, shift until you are balanced.

This is what happens:

You release the pouch. As the stone starts to drop, your throwing hand starts it swinging down across the front of your body. Your throwing hand keeps moving until it is extended to the rear, away from the target.

The pouch is really moving now. Your throwing arm brings it up, and at the same time moves back to send the arc of the pouch up to its highest point behind your head.

Since the pouch is swinging on a string, it will follow an arc. You can't stop it. You can only direct it. Your throwing arm keeps moving back until it is in about the same position it would be in for any full-powered overhand throw.

And that's what you do. The pouch is in position. You bring it forward, high in the air over your throwing shoulder, twisting your body as

you do so. This part of the sequence is almost exactly like serving a tennis ball.

The rest is timing, which comes only with practice. You release the knotted string and the stone whistles away. It really whistles, too, in a hard throw. You can see that there is only one point in any throw where the sling can be released and have the stone strike the target. This point can only be found by "feel," with practice.

Now, what have you done? You've swung the sling in a pattern that takes it from in front of you to behind you, in order to get it into throwing position. That's all. It's far more complicated to describe than it is to do.

Your forward hand remains extended. You use it for balance. With practice you can feel the moment when all your weight and strength should go into the throw, when balance will be needed most. That moment is when the stone in the pouch is through the maneuver that brings it behind you, and is ready to start its upward flight across your shoulder and down. This is where it gains its greatest momentum.

Study the illustrations. See where the stone goes. Then try it until you get the feel of the motion. The rest is practice. Don't discourage too easily. Some people get the hang of it on the first or second try. Others have to work at it.

Keep the problem in mind: The stone is in front of you, and you want it behind you in position for throwing.

Arm and eye must coordinate. This comes with time and practice. Once you know how to get the stone out and far away, accuracy becomes the goal. For accuracy, it's only necessary to have the sling moving in exactly the right direction, and for you to release at exactly the right time. That's all. And a couple of brushes and some paint are all that's necessary to paint a masterpiece, too. Accuracy is about fifty percent practice, and fifty percent natural coordination. Go to it!

You may hear comments and even see pictures of slingmen whirling the gadget around their heads like a Gaucho's bolas. Don't do it. This can fracture skulls and break property. This, or any other improper use of the sling, could result in your sling being burned in a public ceremony while the neighbors chant a ritual song to the effect that you're a menace to the community and a real gone meathead besides. Be careful.

Now, one more step. The staff sling is easier to use, gives greater distance, and takes a larger missile. It is even more dangerous in careless hands.

(These repeated warnings may seem monotonous, but heed them. A sling can be as dangerous

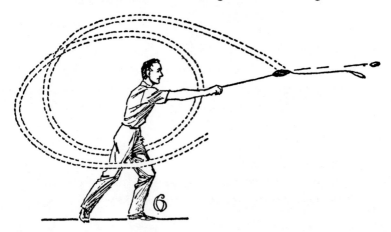

to the person behind the slingman as to the one in front.)

To make a staff sling, make a heavier and larger pouch with stronger cord. The cord can be somewhat longer, too, but start with the same length cord as for the hand sling until you get the skill you need for longer cords. Except for size, the staff sling is identical.

The staff is best cut from a green sapling about an inch in diameter. It should be straight, and of a good wood. Ash, hickory, birch or any similar tough and flexible wood will do. Peel the sapling and use your arm to measure it. Cut it off at arm length.

THE STAFF SLING

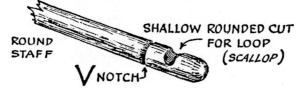

ROUND STAFF

SHALLOW ROUNDED CUT FOR LOOP (SCALLOP)

V NOTCH

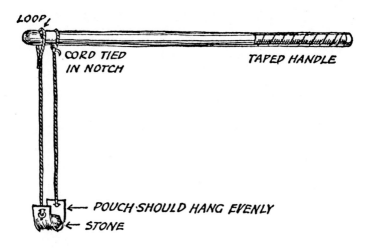

LOOP

CORD TIED IN NOTCH

TAPED HANDLE

← POUCH SHOULD HANG EVENLY

← STONE

Cut a groove around the smaller end, about an inch from the end. Then, between the groove and the end cut out a scallop, as shown in the illustration.

One end of the sling is tied in the groove. The other end is looped, so that it fits loosely over the knob you've created by cutting a scallop.

To use, put a stone in the pouch. Lay the staff over your shoulder, holding it about level. The knob should be upward. Get a grip on the staff like your grip on a baseball bat—firm, but comfortable.

Feet apart and braced, eye on target, and bring the staff forward in the same whipping motion you'd use to drive a stake in the ground in front of you.

If all has gone well, the loop slipped over the knob at the proper point and the stone is on its way. If not, whittle the knob down just a little and try again. Keep experimenting until you get it right. There are no rules, no measurements. It's an individual matter.

Warn the neighbors. Send word to all rabbits to clear the area, and start practicing. Good luck to you!

It's too bad that no further reading can be suggested, because the literature of the sling is pretty scanty.

However, if you're the careless type, do read up on first aid. Then you can treat the unhappy victim while you're explaining how it all happened.

Chapter III

Diving to Fun and Adventure

The barracuda hovered, waiting. Rick knew that its apparent disinterest could change to lightning flight. Few fish are so fast. Flippers propelling him gently, he closed. The barracuda's head was squarely in his sights. Rick squeezed the trigger.

For a moment he thought he had missed, then the safety line ran out and the jerk almost pulled the gun from his hands. He was running out of breath, too. Quickly he planed for the surface, feeling the fury on the end of his line. He broke water, gulped air, then dove again.

from THE WAILING OCTOPUS
Chapter VII, *The Derelict.*

THERE IS a strange and exciting world waiting below the surface of the water. This world is ready for you, just as soon as you're ready for it.

Explaining the thrill of skin diving is difficult. Wonderful descriptions have been written by famous divers, some of whose books are listed at the end of this chapter. But no book can tell all the story. Movies and TV shows can't really explain it either, because you're watching and not actually experiencing the subsurface world. It's as difficult as explaining a rainbow to a color-blind person.

The only satisfactory way to find out what the underwater realm is like is to go and see. To do this requires knowledge and equipment.

As readers of Rick Brant's adventures know, Rick and Scotty find fun and adventure under the water, but they are never careless about equipment or thoughtless in their approach to the underwater world.

Skin diving is for thoughtful sportsmen who are prepared and equipped. It is not for others. The underwater world is safe and pleasant only for those who obey its rules.

You may have thought about skin diving, but decided it was not for you because you don't live near the seashore or a large lake. Great bodies of water aren't necessary. There are rivers and small lakes and ponds scattered across the face of our country. Even the smallest body of water, if it has depths over your head, is a worthy waterland for the skin diver.

Fresh water usually has limitations for spear fishing. In some states it is forbidden entirely, on the grounds that spearfishing is somehow unsporting, and spearfishermen kill more fish than their share. Neither of these views is correct. The spearfisherman works harder for his fish than the angler, and he gets fewer fish—he just has more fun. But a few poor sportsmen have given a wrong impression that it will take years to correct. Perhaps someday game fishing by skin divers will be allowed.

But fresh water has creatures other than fish, ranging from fresh-water sponges that few people have seen to crayfish, crawfish, or crawdads—whatever they call them in your part of the country.

The best way to find out what local waters have to offer is to go and see. You'll be surprised at what a small pond can offer. The author once counted eleven kinds of fish, crayfish, fresh-water mussels, seven kinds of underwater plants and an underwater depository for used tires, all in a little Connecticut lake a few hundred yards long and perhaps 300 yards wide. In this same lake, a 20-minute skin diving expedition once netted four good fishing lures, about a thousand feet of excellent monofilament fishing line, seven punctured beach balls and a pair of old sneakers (wrong size).

The first thing you'll need is a buddy. The buddy system makes good sense in swimming. It's even more essential in diving, if that's possible. Your buddy must be someone you can trust, because your life may depend on his watchfulness and skill. He must be at least as good a swimmer as you are.

After a while you and your buddy will form a natural team. You won't feel comfortable going into the water without him, even if you're foolish enough to do so.

A part of working together is to be able to communicate underwater. There are two ways of doing this, one by hand and arm signals, the other by making sounds. Hand signals are pretty well standardized now. Those in common use are shown in the illustrations.

Sometimes, though, you need your buddy in a hurry when he doesn't happen to be looking at you. It's too much to expect buddies to watch each other all the time. You can't get much exploring done while gazing worriedly into each other's masks, so the hand signals should be supplemented by sounds.

Even though the two of you are searching the bottom or chasing a perch, you should never be out of sight of each other. Check frequently, and keep your ears tuned for sounds when you're not actually looking.

The SCUBA diver has an advantage here, because he has a steel tank on which to hammer. Such a

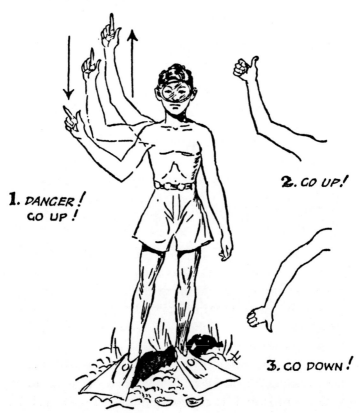

1. DANGER!
   GO UP!

2. GO UP!

3. GO DOWN!

sound can be heard for long distances. But the
SCUBA diver also has a disadvantage. Because of the
sound of his exhaust bubbling, he can hear well
only between breaths. So, for SCUBA, sounds have
to be continuous, a series of bangs on the tank over
a period of a minute or two.

4. *HOLD STILL !*
ONE OR BOTH ARMS
AT 90° ANGLE WITH
FISTS CLENCHED

5. *EVERYTHING O.K!*
THUMB AND FIRST
FINGER FORM CIRCLE

6. *HELP ME !*
RIGHT ARM HELD
STRAIGHT UP, PALM
OUT-- *MOTIONLESS .!*

The skin diver is silent, and so is the world
around him. He can be heard if he hoots. Let's
assume that you're under water with your snorkel
mouthpiece gripped firmly between your teeth.
You're not breathing; it's there for use when you

surface and blow it clear of water. You'll find that by talking in a loud voice, without moving your lips or teeth, you can make effective hooting sounds. It's like imitating a train whistle. Sounds should be simple. Work out your own code for attracting your buddy's attention. Just don't try to breathe while making the sounds.

No matter how expert you get, don't go into the water without your buddy. It's seldom that a diver with a good buddy gets into trouble he can't get out of. Usually it's the lone diver, or the one with an inexperienced or careless buddy, that gets into real danger.

Work as a team. If skin diving without SCUBA, take turns. One dives while the other watches him through his face mask. Take turns leading and following when diving together.

Next comes an understanding of what you're getting into—namely, water. Water has weight. The deeper you go, the more water there is above you to force its weight on you. Since this weight is all around you, pressing from all sides, it's called pressure. Fresh water weighs about 62½ pounds per cubic foot. Sea water weighs about 64 pounds.

Air has weight, too. At sea level, the atmosphere is pressing on every inch of your body, and on every inch of water surface, too, with a weight of 14.7 pounds. One square inch of water at a depth of 33 feet has the same weight—or pressure. So, if you dive to 33 feet, you have one atmosphere of pressure, plus an additional atmosphere of water pressing on every square inch of your body. This adds up to 29.4 pounds. Usually one atmosphere of pressure is rounded off to 15 pounds per square inch for rough figuring. Each 33 feet of depth equals one atmosphere of pressure. This works out to two atmospheres or 30 pounds at 33 feet, three atmospheres or 60 pounds at 66 feet, four atmospheres or 90 pounds at 99 feet, and so on.

Two atmospheres doesn't sound like much,

GRAPH OF PRESSURE INCREASE WITH WATER DEPTH

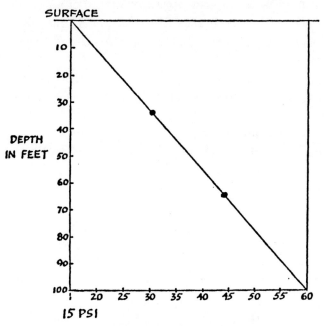

APPROXIMATE PRESSURE IN
POUNDS PER SQUARE INCH (PSI)

TO FIND THE WATER PRESSURE AT ANY DEPTH GO DOWN THE LEFT HAND COLUMN TO THE DEPTH, THEN ACROSS UNTIL THE SLANTING LINE IS REACHED, THEN GO DOWN AND READ THE PRESSURE FROM THE BOTTOM LINE but if you want to see what these figures really mean to a diver, take the area of your chest in square inches and multiply by pounds per square inch. Suppose your chest area is about a foot square. This is 144 square inches. Two atmospheres is about 30 pounds per square inch.

Go ahead and dive. Then surface and brag to your friends, "Why, I actually held over two tons on my chest! It was 4,320 pounds, to be exact."

Don't bother to point out that your chest carries a ton of atmospheric pressure all the time.

Water also is practically incompressible. But if water can't be compressed, gases can—and that includes air.

When diving, we have air or gas space within certain of our tissues and body cavities. The largest space, of course, is our lungs. We also have air space in stomach and intestines, at least most of the time. Our heads are less than solid, too. When you call a fellow diver a bonehead, make allowances for the fact that, like you, he has sinuses, a middle ear, and a Eustachian tube. If you must be

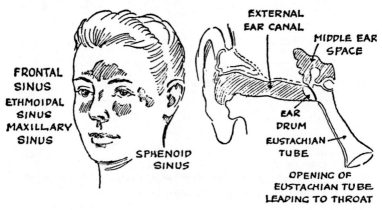

FRONTAL SINUS
ETHMOIDAL SINUS
MAXILLARY SINUS
SPHENOID SINUS

EXTERNAL EAR CANAL
MIDDLE EAR SPACE
EAR DRUM
EUSTACHIAN TUBE
OPENING OF EUSTACHIAN TUBE LEADING TO THROAT

unmannerly, at least call him a perforated bone-head for the sake of scientific accuracy.

All sinuses have openings though which air can pass, unless they are blocked by an infection or the swollen membranes that come with a cold. Our inner ears communicate with the outer air via the Eustachian tube, located down behind your soft palate.

Ever descend rapidly in an elevator or plane, or down a mountain in a car, and feel pressure on your ears? What happened has a bearing on diving. The Eustachian tube is much like a drinking straw with a chewed end. You can blow air through it from the good end, but when you put the chewed end in the glass and try to suck up more soda, the soda won't pass through.

In the same way, as you ascended by plane, elevator or car into thinner air, the excess pressure in your inner ear leaked out so smoothly you never noticed. But on the way down into denser air, your Eustachian tube wouldn't let air pass in quite so easily. The pressure you felt was your eardrums reacting to unequal air pressure—dense air outside, thinner air inside.

Diving is no different, except that you go more rapidly into higher pressure. In this case the pressure is that of water. To equalize pressure in your inner ear, air from your lungs must get through your Eustachian tube. It can't, if you have a cold or infection—at least not rapidly enough. If the outside pressure becomes great enough, you get intense pain in your eardrums. More pressure and the eardrum may rupture.

If this happens, cold water floods into the inner ear. Your body is warm, and the water is cold. This temperature difference completely upsets the balance mechanism in your ear. You get an extreme attack of dizziness, of the kind called

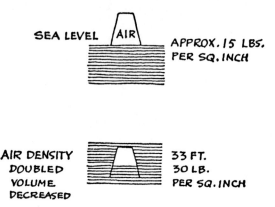

vertigo. It's not uncommon to lose sense of direction completely. The diver doesn't even know where the surface is. He may get sick to his stomach.

A buddy is mighty handy in such cases; lives have been saved by an alert buddy when an eardrum gave way.

A SCUBA diver has an advantage in such a case. He has air. He can wait, hugging himself or a nearby object until the water in his inner ear is warmed up. Then the vertigo leaves and he can find his way again. But a snorkel diver usually can't wait that long. He must surface to breathe.

The action of pressure on air and other gases is described by what is known as Boyle's Law. It states that, at a constant temperature, the volume of a gas varies inversely as the absolute pressure, and the density varies directly as the pressure. This means simply that, if the pressure on a gas is doubled, the density also is doubled—but the volume is reduced to one half.

You're at 33 feet below the water. The pressure on your chest is double that of the one atmosphere of pressure at the surface. The pressure on the air in your lungs is also doubled, but the volume of air is decreased by half.

You filled your lungs before you dived, so your lungs are now half full. This is still enough air for your dive, even though it's compressed air now. If you could dive deep enough, the volume of air in your lungs would decrease even beyond the point you reach when you breathe out as completely as you can. Your chest muscles could still handle this by collapsing inward naturally. But deeper still, and the water pressure could fracture ribs. Don't worry about this, though. You won't dive that deep; you can't, without weights, which skin divers do not use.

The real problem is your sinuses. The volume of air in the sinus cavities is also reduced by half. This leaves, in effect, a partial vacuum. If you are completely healthy, air from your lungs will make up the difference. But if the air passages are blocked by infection or swollen membranes from a cold, no air can get in. The delicate tissues that line the sinus cavities collapse into the cavities, rupturing in the process. This may not hurt at the time. Many a diver who violated Boyle's Law with a cold in the head knew nothing of it until he surfaced and found his mask full of blood.

This can happen even with care, and it is not a matter for real anxiety. The doctor will know what to do, and it will probably mean only complete lack of diving for some time. But don't risk it. If you have any doubts at all about ears, nose or sinuses, have a physical examination before you start diving. Most clubs require a complete physical and all YMCA courses do. It's good sense.

One interesting side effect of water pressure is that chest muscles can't act effectively against it unless compressed air is fed, on demand, to the lungs. A man six feet under water can't breathe at all through an open tube to the surface. At lesser depths he can breathe with great and tiring effort. Even a foot of water makes hard work. This fact of pressure puts a wet and dismal blanket across the favorite movie and TV scene where the hero hides in a swamp, breathing through a hollow reed. Sorry. Won't work, Joe. Better keep running.

A snorkel is a breathing tube for use on the surface. Your face is less than six inches under and your chest only a little more. Yet, extended use of a snorkel will leave you pretty tired. Some divers don't know this, and wonder why they tire out just floating around on the surface, snorkeling happily and watching the fish.

A diver must be an excellent swimmer. This is hard to believe when beginners put on swimming aids and go blithely off into the drink with no trouble at all. With mask, snorkel and flippers even a non-swimmer can look like a champ, until he accidently dunks his snorkel under the water and gulps a snootful. Then he'd better have help on hand in a hurry, or the National Safety Council will have another statistic.

Swimming and diving is easy with aids when all is going smoothly. Only, underwater, nothing goes smoothly for the beginner. Things are smooth for the expert only because he is an expert. He can handle himself in the water. He doesn't panic. The small troubles, like a maskful of water, a lost fin, or a snorkel that's dunked by a wave are handled so effortlessly that the diver doesn't even think about it.

The Scripps Institute of Oceanography, in La Jolla, California, puts diver candidates through a test. Could you pass it?

1. Swim 1,000 feet without fins, in the ocean.
2. Swim in a rip current.
3. Swim underwater a distance of 75 feet, without fins and without surfacing.
4. Skin dive to a depth of 18 feet.
5. Skin dive to a depth of 10 feet and recover another diver.
6. Tow a swimmer 75 feet on the surface.
7. Give artificial respiration by the method taught by the Red Cross (which all divers should know).

This is pretty stiff. A somewhat easier but adequate test is given by the Los Angeles Lifeguard Service:

1. Swim 200 yards without swim aids.
2. Swim 10 yards underwater without aids.
3. Swim 50 yards with 10 pounds of weight. (iron or lead in a belt)
4. Tread water for five minutes.
5. Tread water with hands out of the water for 30 seconds.

These examples will show you how good a swimmer you must be. If there is a club or YMCA course near you, you will be given a test. If not, give yourself one. If you want to start off right, get a Red Cross Water Safety Card. It will prove to you that experts agree that you can handle yourself in the water. Ask your local chapter.

Now, you have a buddy, a place to swim, and ability to take care of yourself in the water. You need equipment. Don't be hasty in buying it. Study the equipment in the stores, but unless you know that the clerk is a diver himself, take what he says with a grain of salt—or a shakerful. The following item-by-item discussion will serve as a guide.

THE MASK

Human eyes were not made for underwater vision. We see dimly, and not in focus. But the moment a layer of air is added, we can see very well, although there is distortion of size and distance. The first time you examine your feet underwater through a face mask you'll wonder if they belong to you. One gets used to this, though, and allows for it in reaching for an object. Still, it's sad to see the biggest whatnot ever captured underwater shrink to pretty small size when taken to the surface.

This distortion is why fish stories by divers must be discounted. That "enormous" shark probably would fit comfortably into the guppy tank in some cases.

TYPES OF MASKS

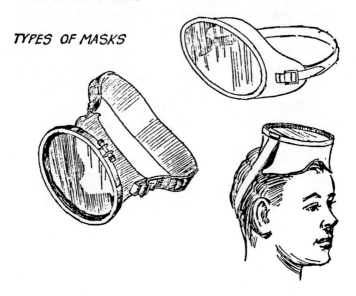

Goggles put a layer of air between eyes and water, but remember Boyle's Law. Dive with goggles and the volume of air is dimished. The only thing that can fill the partial vacuum—or, more accurately, the pressure imbalance—is your own tissue. Bulging eyes is the least you can expect from a deep dive. Leave the goggles to the kids in the paddle pond.

With a mask the volume of air is also reduced,

but the mask covers your nose. Exhaling into the mask equalizes the pressure. But do not use a mask that covers mouth as well as nose for skin diving. Some SCUBAS have masks that cover the entire face, but this is different, since the air supply is built in.

Masks can be made, but in these days of cheap plastic it actually costs more to make a poor and leaky one than to buy a cheap model. In season, masks can be bought at drug stores for a dollar or less.

Cheap masks are not ideal by any means, but they're a whole lot better than nothing. The main disadvantages are that they are usually made of a fairly stiff plastic that chafes the face, the plastic face plates get scratched easily or become murky from chemical reactions in the water, and they don't last nearly as long as a good mask. But if you can do no better, make sure at least that the mask fits. Put it on, and inhale, through your nose. If the mask fits, you will feel it being sucked into your face. Keep trying until you get a fit. If a cheap one is all you can afford, if it won't fit and you're desperate, a round section of inner tube can be glued to the mask skirt with plenty of good cement and trimmed until the soft rubber fits your face contours.

The ideal mask has a soft skirt that molds neatly to your face, and the bands that hold it to your head are firm but comfortable. The plate is of clear safety glass, not plastic.

There are many sizes and shapes of mask. Choose those with clear glass and try them on until you find the one that feels best.

If you can't get safety glass, get plastic. The principal disadvantage of plastic is that it scratches easily. Next in importance is that it fogs up as the moisture from your breath condenses. About the only way to keep a plastic plate clear is to have a little water in the mask. The water can be swished across the face plate by turning your head. That will keep the fog cleared up.

With a safety glass plate, spit on the plate and then rinse. It will stay clear. Safety glass also resists scratches.

Masks come with both clear and tinted face plates. An amber tint helps slightly, but it's mostly a matter of choice.

Those who wear glasses can get masks that will take an insert into which prescription lenses can be fitted. Most glasses wearers can probably do without glasses. Or, if a little water leakage isn't bothersome, glasses with thin bows can be worn right under the mask. Try and see if this works for you. Some people have trouble, others don't.

Masks also come with built-in snorkels. The snorkels have automatic closing devices that usually work by gravity—which means little when a diver is upside down. A maskful of water isn't uncommon with these, but perhaps experience will show that you prefer one.

Clearing the mask of water while submerged is a trick you should know, and it's not difficult. Air is lighter than water, so you clamp the *upper* part of your mask to your face to keep the air in, then snort air into the mask through your nose. If you hold the *bottom* part of your mask slightly away from your face, the air from your nose will force

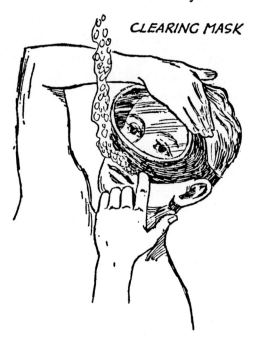

CLEARING MASK

the water out. The only trick to it is applying the pressure properly. Practice until you get it, then continue to practice until you can clear your mask with one good snort.

SNORKEL

The purpose of a snorkel is to allow a diver to float face down on the surface, watching the water and bottom under him without the necessity of turning his head to breathe. This purpose is the only one—but it certainly makes the snorkel worth while.

Snorkels come in all sorts of shapes and sizes. Avoid the very long ones, otherwise choose the one you like.

The snorkel preferred by most experienced divers is flexible, simply a pipe of rubber or plastic with a U shape on the bottom and a mouthpiece. Another kind that some divers like goes from mouth straight up past the middle of the face plate and anchors to a small nut and bolt that holds the stainless steel rim around the mask.

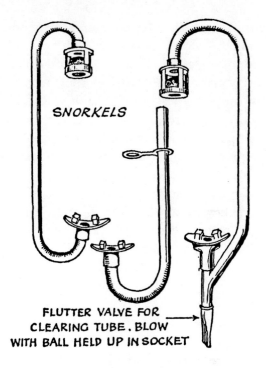

SNORKELS

FLUTTER VALVE FOR
CLEARING TUBE. BLOW
WITH BALL HELD UP IN SOCKET

Some snorkels come equipped with a rubber band that goes around the head. Others have a small tab with a slot through which a band of the face mask is slipped. The snorkel then stays on the mask.

Many divers use no snorkel strap at all. When

diving, they thrust the snorkel through their belts.

Like masks, snorkels come in many types and prices. The cheap ones sold in drug stores are about as good as the expensive ones. A saw will remove the upper U and give you a straight pipe if you prefer.

FINS

Fins are called different names, depending on location and local practice. They're swim fins, flippers, webfeet, duckfeet, and so on. But a fin by any other name would work as well. Your legs are one of the most powerful parts of your body, but in swimming they don't have enough surface to put the power to efficient use. Fins simply add to the amount of surface, at the point of greatest leverage.

The most important thing in selecting fins is the fit. They should be snug, but not tight. Since you're most likely still growing, the fins with adjustable heel straps are most sensible for you, even though they're not as comfortable as the slipper kind that fits your foot perfectly.

Giant-size flippers can be bought, but keep away from them until you're a veteran. They're too tiring for the beginner, and a little harder to control than the normal size.

The best fins are flexible, but not floppy. If too rigid, they may chafe.

As in mask and snorkel buying, do the best your budget allows.

Remember that even the cheapest equipment will give lots of satisfaction. The best equipment will make diving more comfortable, and it will last longer. That's about the main difference.

Fins for the hands are sold, too. You don't need them. In skin diving, the hands are tools and not aids in swimming.

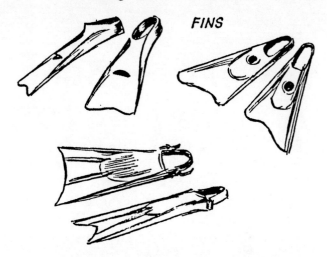

FINS

Use of the fins is natural and easy. Your legs move in a rhythmic flutter kick, knees slightly bent. No need of pounding your legs up and down, either. Just a natural, easy motion from the hips does the trick, and you glide through the water like a porpoise. Your arms hang down, or you fold them across your chest or just use them for feelers in front of you.

Ready to dive? You're face down in the water. Bend in the middle, letting head and upper body go under. As you start to go down throw your legs straight up. Then, as you feel your flippers go under, start your flutter kick. You're on your way with no splash, scarcely a ripple behind you.

EAR PLUGS

Never, never, a thousand times never, use ear plugs. They trap air between themselves and the eardrum. Remember Boyle's Law? When this air is compressed it can only be filled by your eardrum itself. If you're lucky, you'll only experience great pain. If you have sensitive ears, don't try ear plugs—just forget diving. It's not for you.

KNIFE

A good knife is a handy tool. There are fancy knives available for plenty of hard cash, but they're more ornamental than useful. The best diver's knife has a tough blade that can be used for prying; it has a regular cutting edge on the bottom and a sawtooth serrated edge on top.

Divers almost never use knives for fighting sharks or for anything similar. They use knives for collecting specimens, for cutting themselves loose from rope or kelp or for spearing the wily hot dog during the weiner roast after the dive.

A cheap knife for cleaning fish is sold in many places. It has the cutting edge and the saw edge, but is not very tough. Still, it's better than most of the fancy Arkansas toothpicks sold. It will rust easily, so clean, dry and oil after every use.

Keep your knife in a sheath. Some divers pack their sheaths with waterproof grease. Then the knife is waterproofed at all times except when in use.

Just remember that only an ignorant movie hero ever holds his knife with the blade pointing down away from the thumb. Hold the knife like a sword, or as though you were carving the Sunday roast. Keep this in mind when placing the sheath on your belt. You'll probably end up with it across your body from the hand that uses it, or at an angle in the middle of your back. This latter is a good place, because the knife is out of the way.

FLOATS

The float can be a diver's best friend. When you're tired and a long way from shore, that old inner tube is a great comfort. If you fish, it's very important. It is not a good idea to carry bloody fish around in the ocean. The shark might not distinguish between you and your game.

The least expensive float, and the most popular, is an automobile inner tube. One too patched for the car is still good enough, so long as the patches are sound and the valve tight.

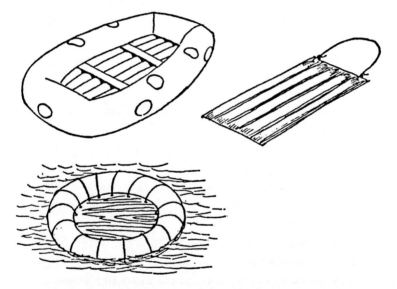

Sometimes a piece of marine or exterior grade plywood is cut in a circle to fit the bottom, and then lashed to the tube with turns of rope that go through holes in the rim of the plywood, around the tube, back through another hole, and so on.

A line to connect you to the float is needed. A

loose float floats—off beyond reach when you most need it.

One-man surplus life rafts are popular. So are rubber or plastic mattresses. There are super extra special 100 percent terrific floats made just for skin divers, too, and some of them are just as good as an old inner tube. But get a float. You'll need one.

BELT

A belt is handy for holding up trunks, which may have a tendency to slip off during a fast dive. This can cause considerable consternation. But a belt is also handy for other things, like carrying a knife sheath, providing a place to hook a float line, or to hang a hank of rope.

A surplus military belt is a good kind, and most of the pouches, sheaths and so on that you might need are available with fittings for the belt.

Any stout cloth belt will do, too. Leather softens and gives up after a few dives. A woven belt of nylon would be excellent—if you can weave, make one.

Never hang weights on your belt. Never!

The SCUBA diver needs a weighted belt to just balance his bouyancy, but he must use a belt with a positive quick release that can be snapped open with one hand in pitch blackness while Creatures from the Dark Lagoon menace him—if he ever gets into such a mess. The belt and weights *must* drop off instantly when he needs to lighten weight. Nothing less will do; it could mean his life. If you can afford SCUBA, you can afford a good belt, for weights only. Your skin-diving belt will do for other things.

PROTECTIVE SUITS

The cold-water diver is known by his toughness, measured by the altitude of his goose pimples. But for those who like comfort with their diving, cold water need not be cause for misery. Cold water is not only uncomfortable, it's exhausting. Your body can't keep up with the heat loss.

There are two kinds of protective suit: wet and dry.

Dry suits are supposed to keep all water out but seldom do. They cover you from neck to hoof, with a watertight hood to match. Underwear—longies—is worn under a dry suit, to provide insulation. Dry suits are the most satisfactory, and most expensive.

Wet suits get wet. They trap a layer of water next to your skin. The layer of water is warmed by your body, and provides insulation from the cold. Wet suits are often made of foam neoprene. Often they are worn in pieces—jersey top for mildly cold water, shorts when temperatures demand, or whole suits complete with socks and hood, to be put on a piece at a time. Wet suits are less expensive, but not cheap.

Even if you can't afford a suit, you need not brave the dank and dismal cold with only your skin and trunks. Other garments are helpful. A suit of long underwear also traps a layer of water next to your skin, but doesn't hold it as well. A suit of longies dipped in liquid latex makes a pretty good wet suit.

A woolen sweater helps protect your upper body. A turtleneck sweater is the best kind for this purpose. A sweat shirt is helpful, too, although it gets pretty heavy when wet, and it sags. Even a T shirt helps in milder weather.

Gym socks on your feet will help keep them warm, but allow room in your flippers. Let out the straps if you have the adjustable kind.

If you're not bashful, borrow your sister's leotard-type garments and put your trunks on over them. If they're green, you'll look like Robin Hood. If red, like the Scarlet Pimpernel. If black, like Captain John Smith. If pink, better forget the whole thing. A bass might mistake you for a chrysanthemum.

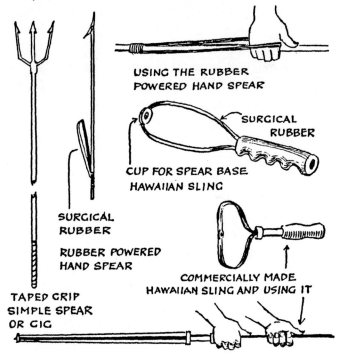

USING THE RUBBER POWERED HAND SPEAR

SURGICAL RUBBER

CUP FOR SPEAR BASE
HAWAIIAN SLING

SURGICAL RUBBER

RUBBER POWERED HAND SPEAR

COMMERCIALLY MADE HAWAIIAN SLING AND USING IT

TAPED GRIP
SIMPLE SPEAR
OR GIG

SPEARS AND GUNS

Check the game laws for your state. If spear-fishing is allowed, start with a simple hand spear. Then graduate to a spear with rubber propulsion. Then to a Hawaiian sling. A rubber powered gun is next. If you're a good handyman, you can make your own gun. Some of the books at the end of the chapter tell you how.

GLOVES

Gloves are a good idea, especially in the ocean. Barnacles cut and coral hurts. Use work gloves, but get the closely woven kind.

SCUBA

SCUBA stands for Self-Contained Underwater Breathing Apparatus.

The original SCUBA was the aqualung, with the valve invented by Costeau and Gagnon, in France. Now there are many SCUBAS on the market, ranging in price from less than forty dollars to several hundred. They use a variety of principles, but all work on the demand principle—that is, they give the diver the amount of air he needs at the pressure he needs, and they do it automatically. All the diver has to do is breathe.

There is no room in a single chapter for a long discussion of SCUBA. A few things, however, need to be said.

Use *only* the SCUBA that contains compressed air. So-called "closed circuit" SCUBAS use only oxygen. But oxygen, the life giver, is a poison when breathed pure at more than two atmospheres of pressure. It is not for skin divers. Stay away from it.

Avoid "surplus" or "modified" regulators. Some of them work, but only a real mechanical expert can tell which ones are safe. Use only regulators (demand valves) made expressly for scuba diving.

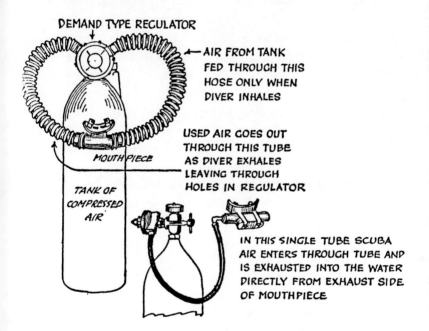

DEMAND TYPE REGULATOR

← AIR FROM TANK FED THROUGH THIS HOSE ONLY WHEN DIVER INHALES

USED AIR GOES OUT THROUGH THIS TUBE AS DIVER EXHALES LEAVING THROUGH HOLES IN REGULATOR

MOUTHPIECE

TANK OF COMPRESSED AIR

IN THIS SINGLE TUBE SCUBA AIR ENTERS THROUGH TUBE AND IS EXHAUSTED INTO THE WATER DIRECTLY FROM EXHAUST SIDE OF MOUTHPIECE

Anyone can buy or rent a scuba, put it on and dive smoothly into the depths. This is done every day. But in spite of simplicity of operation, scuba requires expert instruction, good knowledge of the principles of diving, and plenty of practice.

The happy amateur who uses one without instruction is apt to be a real gone gosling if even the slightest mishap occurs, like losing the mouthpiece. Even experts let their mouthpieces slip out of place. The difference is that they get them back in again without taking on a lungful of water.

Read Chapter VI in the ELECTRONIC MIND READER, and see how Rick puts Jan Miller through her final SCUBA test. Only when you can pass such a test are you ready for SCUBA diving.

SCUBA costs quite a bit. But even if you can't afford your own, you may be able to SCUBA dive through clubs.

There are diving clubs in every state, most of them helpful to beginners. Many clubs own equipment for the use of members, and nearly all give instruction. Many local YMCA's now sponsor clubs or have SCUBA courses. Check around. If your library subscribes to *Skin Diver Magazine,* check back-issues for news of clubs in your vicinity. Good luck!

Once you're on the way, the underwater world is yours. Depending on where you live, the kind of water near you and your own inclinations, you can spearfish, explore wrecks, go in for underwater nature study—which is most satisfying for the scientifically inclined and curious diver—and even earn money if you're lucky.

Boys can earn money diving because of the careless habits of boating enthusiasts. Many an outboarder forgets to secure his motor, which works off the transom and plunges to the bottom. Many a boater loses stuff overboard, ranging in size from people to sunglasses. The log of the author's cruiser *Spindrift* contains a full page of stuff dropped overboard, only about half of it recovered. The rest is small stuff, lost forever in the ooze at the bottom of Chesapeake Bay.

When you become expert and you've practiced rope work and recovery of objects, arrange with local boating clubs and docks to post a notice on the bulletin board:

LOST OBJECTS RECOVERED BY EXPERT
DIVERS. DON'T BEAT YOUR HEAD AGAINST
THE GUNWALE. USE IT TO CALL THE
DIVING TWINS. PHONE DUNKUM 0–0000.

There are excellent books on skin diving. Your librarian probably has a number. Study them, then join a club if you can. If not, work slowly and carefully with your buddy on the fundamentals.

Remember, it's a safe sport for the diver who uses his head. Don't be a glubber—be a diver.

Try these books:

Underwater Safety Manual, published by the Aquatics Division of the Los Angeles County Department of Parks and Recreation. Write and inquire. This is a first-rate book.

Underwater, by Bill Barada. Good reading, short, but with useful hints and how-to-do-it sketches.

Dive, by Rick and Barbara Carrier. Excellent and detailed.

The Silent World, by Jacques Yves Costeau. This is a book of the author's adventures in the early days of skin diving. Costeau is the co-inventor of the famed aqualung, and the father of modern SCUBA diving. Great reading. It made a magnificent movie, too.

The Skin Diver Magazine, a monthly devoted to the sport published in Lynwood, California. Good for the ads, among other things. Helps to keep up with new equipment.

And for a boy's eye view of fun and adventure underwater, Rick and Scotty dive in both THE WAILING OCTOPUS and THE ELECTRONIC MIND READER.

Chapter IV

Exploring the Microworld

Rick focused the microscope on the drop of water. Yesterday the rock basin had been literally aswarm with paramecia and other forms of life. Today, the water from the basin was as devoid of life as the planet Jupiter.

Rick shook his head in bewilderment. "Whatever the Blue Ghost is," he stated, "it's a killer. The mob we saw is gone."

from THE BLUE GHOST MYSTERY
Chapter VI, *The Lifeless Water*

THE "MOB" to which Rick Brant refers in the story of the Blue Ghost is a teeming horde of monsters, but of a kind seldom seen in horror movies for the good reason that they're invisible to the naked eye.

This doesn't mean that some producer won't some day focus a camera through a microscope in order to find a new kind of villain. If this should happen, the advertising for the picture is easy to predict:

THE MONSTER WITH THE BUZZSAW MOUTH! SEE THE HORROR FROM THE SWAMP AS IT MENACES THE WORLD WITH VAST, SNAKELIKE TENTACLES.

When this ad appears you can nod your head

sagely, recognizing the monster as a rotifer, of the kind called Stephenoceros.

THE MONSTER WITH THE BUZZSAW MOUTH

Another fascinating creature that would make a good horror movie candidate is hydra. This one looks like a child's drawing of a tree, but it's an animal just the same. It eats other animals of its own size or even larger. Cut it to pieces and new individuals sprout from the chunks. Tear it limb from limb and a whole new colony of horrors is created.

Come to think of it, it's a good thing for us that the microscopic creatures aren't our size. Not only are they savage, but they outnumber us.

All this is by way of introduction to still another aspect of the underwater world—and to a different view of dry land and its inhabitants, too.

To understand the microworld, we need a window through which our limited eyes can see. Not long ago such windows were too expensive for most people. Low-power lenses for reading were common, and few boys have not used a magnifying glass to concentrate the sun's rays and set paper afire. But such lenses are not powerful enough to look in on the microworld.

During the past decade things have changed greatly. Now the microworld is open to any boy or girl with sufficient pocket money, or the means of making it.

American-made microscopes are on the market, often in sets that contain much of what is needed to explore the microworld. Foreign instruments of several kinds are now widely sold, usually at a lower cost than the American instruments. As good? No, not in the lower price ranges, but they provide a useful window into the microworld just the same.

The microscope is at the end of a long line of magnifiers, ranging in price from a dollar to several, and ranging in magnification power from four or five diameters to nearly a hundred.

Diameters means magnification, but in a precise way. Suppose we assume that the period at the end of this sentence is about a 32nd of an inch in diameter. Under a lens that magnifies eight diameters it will be eight thirtyseconds (8/32nds) or one quarter of an inch in diameter. This is a considerable enlargement.

Diameter means exactly what it says: that the dimensions of an object are apparently increased by the number of diameters at which the lens is rated.

Another way of stating the power of a lens is by the use of x. 4x on a lens means that it enlarges by four diameters.

To begin your exploration of the microworld,

start by making a lens. This sounds pretty tough, but it's actually easy, if you follow on the trail of Leeuwenhoek, the 17th-century Netherlander who is called the Father of the Microscope.

LEEUWENHOEK

The Dutchman laboriously ground lenses of glass, actually glass beads. But you'll use water. Where he used silver plates, you'll use a fine wire or a piece of cardboard.

There are copper wires so fine they seem scarcely larger than threads. If you know an electronics hobbyist, he may have some left over from winding coils. If not, find a length of ordinary lamp cord or extension wire. This kind of wire is made up of many strands of fine wire.

Separate out a two- or three-inch length of the fine wire and straighten it. Then, make a tiny loop in one end as the illustration shows.

To turn the loop into a lens it is only necessary to capture a bubble of water in the loop, by dipping it into water.

Try your homemade lens on a piece of paper. See if the fibers are visible through the center of the water bubble. Arrange the paper on top of a lamp, or a glass table top with a lamp under it.

You may find circles of color in your lens. Leeuwenhoek did, and he got rid of them by making the hole smaller.

As you try out this primitive kind of lens, take a moment to marvel at the Dutchman who made some of the earliest discoveries about the microworld with an instrument not much more advanced than the one you have made. His lens was of glass; he put the object to be studied on a needlepoint, and controlled its distance from the lens with a screw. But his lenses were little different from yours, and his eyes probably no better.

This kind of home experiment is fun to try once, but you want a lens that is more permanent and easier to use than a water bubble.

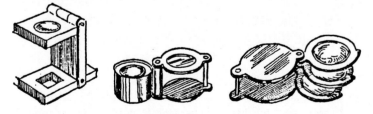

A pocket lens will be useful for many things. Such lenses come in a choice of shapes, sizes and powers. Any optical supply store will be able to show you several.

If possible, get a folding lens, one with a protective case into which the lens folds. A metal case is best. Such lenses cost as little as one dollar, depending on power. The higher the power, the higher the cost—and the smaller the lens. Pocket lenses range up to 30x or even more.

Be sure to try out a lens before you buy. High-power lenses must be *aplanatic,* which means without color. A lens that shows colored rings at the edges is not aplanatic.

(In cameras, telescopes and binoculars, the term *achromatic* means the same thing.)

Glass never wears out, so a pocket lens will last a lifetime if cared for. It will show you fascinating details of such living things as water fleas, the stinging hairs on nettles, the intricate designs in insect wings, the clashing mandibles of fighting ants, and a host of other features invisible to the naked eye.

If you become interested in the microworld, (and you can't look into it without becoming interested) get into the habit of carrying your pocket lens with you. Then, when you come across a strange creature, your instinct will be to examine it—not just to step on it.

There is a kind of pocket lens sold for a rather moderate price, somewhere between three and five dollars, that is actually a microscope. These lenses are advertised as combination telescopes and microscopes.

The telescope part can be discounted. True, they do magnify, but the light-gathering properties are so poor that they have no real value. As a

microscope, however, these instruments are useful. The usual magnifications are 50 and 60 diameters. Of course the ability to carry one in a
pocket is an added value.

Construction of a pocket microscope is the same
as that of any microscope, so far as the optical
system is concerned. The instrument consists of
two tubes, one inside the other. The outer tube
carries a lens at the bottom end. The inner tube
has a lens at the upper end. To focus, the inner
tube is moved up and down. A special metal fitting, highly polished and concave in shape, is
screwed on below the lower lens. In the center of
the fitting is a small hole. Light is concentrated on
the object being inspected by the concave shape.
The object is viewed through the hole.

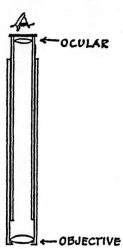

The standard microscope has the same arrangement of sliding tubes, but the inner tube is controlled by a screw arrangement for easier focusing.

The outer tube is attached to a frame. Instead of a concave metallic mirror, the standard instrument has a "stage" on which the specimen rests. There is a hole in the stage. Below the hole is a mirror, or an electric light source to provide illumination.

The lower lens on a microscope is called the *objective*. The upper lens, through which the eye looks, is called the *ocular*. The power of the instrument is the product of the powers of the two lenses. For instance, in a microscope with three objective lenses on a turret, the most common powers are 10x, 20x and 30x. In such an inexpensive microscope the power of the ocular lens is 10x.

With the 10x objective in place, the microscope magnifies by 10x times 10x, or 100 diameters. With the 20x objective in place, the total power is 20x times 10x, or 200x. And so on.

Before putting good money into an instrument, it's best to decide where your interest lies. If you have genuine curiosity about the world in which we live, a microscope offers the best way to look at a very large but invisible part of it.

Of course, if you get an instrument and find that it is not for you, it is very good for trading. You might swap with a misguided archery enthusiast who wanted to be a modern Robin Hood until a bowstring took the skin off his arm. The trading possibilities are just about endless.

But if you turn out to be a genuine, stained-on-the-slide microscopy enthusiast, you can use your instrument in studying insects, soils, fibers of all kinds, the structure of plants, bacteriology, contamination of foods, fingerprint analysis and other scientific detective work, and even the study of blood and tissues.

A fascinating field of research is microsurgery. Three animals that lend themselves to scientific study through surgery techniques are hydra, a tiny flatworm called planaria, and the much used fruit fly of the scientist who specializes in genetics.

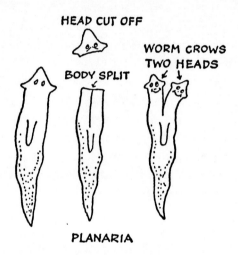

HEAD CUT OFF

WORM GROWS
TWO HEADS

BODY SPLIT

PLANARIA

In microsurgery, the regeneration of parts and organs is the main thing to study. Lop off the head of a planarian and the creature grows a new one. Split him down the middle and he becomes two creatures.

One of the most interesting ventures into the invisible world, however, is keeping a microzoo. Any zoo is interesting, but the average boy's ability to collect enough animals of different species is apt to be limited. With a microzoo, it is possible to have a dozen varieties of animals, some of them pretty fierce and all of them interesting. They can range in size from a few that are just visible to the naked eye to some that can be seen only under the lens.

Comes feeding time at the microzoo, there is no problem. Food is added only occasionally to the water in which the animals are kept. A lot of useful experimenting can be done with foods, too. Some of the common foods for feeding a microzoo are Brewer's Yeast, egg yolk, meat broth and gelatin. A few cents invested in food will keep a whole microzoo for months.

The zoo is kept in jars, each neatly labeled. To inspect the zoo, a well slide is used. The animals are caught in a dip tube, transferred to the well slide and put on the microscope stage. They can then be examined at leisure.

Your zoo cards, which are labels on the jars, might read as follows:

BRINE SHRIMP

These microscopic shrimp were hatched at the zoo. They are useful in feeding baby fish.

PARAMECIA

Also known as "slipper animalcules" because of their shape, paramecia are among the most common of zoo animals.

AMOEBA

This single-cell animal is the remote ancestor of the zoo-keeper.

THE ZOO   AMOEBA

Flagellates

Several species of flagellates are included in the exhibit, including volvox, synura and carteria. These animals whip themselves through the water.

Hydra

Although hydra looks like a plant, it is a carnivorous animal capable of eating creatures larger than itself.

Daphnia

These water fleas are a favorite fish food.

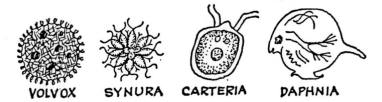

VOLVOX   SYNURA   CARTERIA   DAPHNIA

ROTIFERS

Several species of rotifer may be found in the zoo. These active animals have "wheels" that serve as mouths and as propellers. See the wheels revolve!

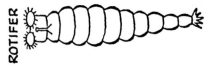

These are only a few. We have not mentioned several protozoa, polyzoa, water bears, rhizopods other than the amoeba, several kinds of water fleas, or several large bacteria.

A microzoo can be supplemented by a microbotanical garden, too, with many interesting microscopic plants, including the diatom that builds itself a shell and sometimes occurs in such great numbers that its shells form a special kind of earth, called diatomaceous earth, invaluable for certain industrial processes.

A microzoo or a microbotanical garden offer possibilities for real research, as well as the fun of collecting and keeping microscopic pets. The life cycles, behavior, feeding habits and other data about many microscopic animals are not well known. You can add to available information and possibly make a genuine scientific contribution.

A primary requirement for a microzoo is, of course, an instrument of sufficient power. Many microscopic animals are visible to low-power lenses, such as we have already discussed. Others need more magnification. Best, of course, is a microscope.

The question is, how much does an instrument cost?

The answer is, from $2.95 up—with emphasis mostly on the "up."

There are two old sayings for shoppers that apply here. First, you get just about what you pay for. Second, as the Romans used to say, *Caveat emptor,* which means, "Let the buyer beware." In other words, a low price means a low quality instrument, and be careful before you make a purchase.

Let's sample the market just to give an idea of costs. *Science News Letter,* a publication of Science Service, Inc., probably can be found in your local library. It carries ads for various kinds of equipment. A sampling of these ads over a period of about six weeks shows the following:

A turret microscope with wooden case, magnifying 100, 200 and 300 diameters, for $6.25.

An 80 to 600x microscope with triple turret and dual eyepiece for $16.95.

A stereoscope (three-dimensional) 30x microscope for $19.95.

A pocket microscope-telescope with 50x magnification when used as a microscope, for $4.50.

In addition there are companies that put out complete microscopy sets, in a whole range of qualities and prices. Such sets may be your best bet. As an example of the range, here are two:

A beginner's set, with triple turret microscope for 40, 75 and 150 diameters, glass slides, specimens and a dissecting kit, for $5.00.

A complete micro-laboratory with a microscope that combines a four-turret lens system with dual eyepieces for magnifications from 75 to 750 diameters, complete laboratory apparatus including a precision microtome—which is a super-sharp controlled knife for slicing specimens to razor thin segments—test tubes, slides, and dissecting equipment. This set also includes a sub-stage light, and a special "electronic" stage for observing atomic disintegrations. The cost is $22.00.

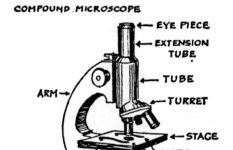

PARTS OF THE
COMPOUND MICROSCOPE

EYE PIECE
EXTENSION TUBE
TUBE
ARM
TURRET
STAGE
CLIPS
JOINT
MIRROR
FOOT

In between these two sets are others at intervals of about five dollars. All sets have instruction manuals, and those over ten dollars come in metal cases.

The cheapest microscope the author has been able to find is a Japanese import for $2.95. It has a triple turret, and magnifications of 100, 200 and 300 diameters.

It works, but little more can be said for it. Certainly it is better than no microscope at all, but the difference between $2.95 and $5.00 is not so great that a little patience, a few more lawns mowed or other chores done for a quarter here and a dime there wouldn't be worth waiting for.

A poor microscope is hard on the eyes, it may not be color corrected, and it may have lens imperfections that will become bothersome. The less you pay for an instrument the more chance you take on getting poor quality. This is natural, since a microscope is a precision instrument that takes time, skilled workmen, and good quality materials to produce.

Get the best microscope you can afford, even if it means waiting until your ready cash builds up. Remember that you're buying something that will not wear out. A good instrument is a lifetime investment.

Like all hobbies, the basic instrument is a beginning. In microscopy, some things must be bought, but others can be made or improvised.

Things to buy are glass slips, cover slips, and balsam. A box of slips will last a long time. These are clear glass rectangles to be used in making slides. Cover slips are glass squares so thin that a hard look will break one. They are also needed in making slides. Balsam is a clear adhesive that smells like a pine forest and is used for securing specimens to slips, and cementing down cover slips to seal the specimen permanently in place. Two ounces of balsam will last for months.

Things you don't need to buy include jars. Every household uses pickles, salad dressings, rel-

ishes and whatnot, all of which come in jars.
Those with screw tops are best, and wide mouths
make them easier to handle.

SLIDE AND SLIP

FLY'S WING
SEALED UNDER
COVER SLIP
WITH BALSAM

The jars can be supplemented by a few pill
bottles, the kind with a plastic snap-on top.

An eye dropper is a useful tool. Most houses
have one or two left over from a cold in the nose,
or an earache. If not, a dime will buy one at the
drug store.

A dip tube is very important, and requires another dime for the purchase of a glass drinking
straw from the drug store. The straw is turned
into a dip tube by heating it in the middle until
soft, then drawing it out.

Best heat comes from a Bunsen burner. If your
school lab has one you can probably arrange to
use it. If not, a gas stove works, too. Don't try to
make a dip tube on an electric range, though.
Melted glass makes an awful mess.

No Bunsen burner and no gas stove? Try a
friendly plumber. The torch or stove he uses for
melting solder will do, and he may heat the tube
for you.

The hot glass is pulled apart, leaving two sections of glass with long points. The points are
broken off, leaving tiny holes. A dip tube is used
by clamping a thumb or finger over the large end

and lowering the pointed end into the water next to the animal to be picked up. When the thumb is removed, water rushes into the tube, probably pulling the animal with it.

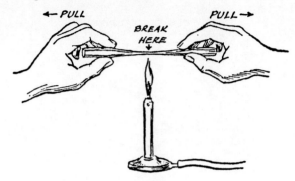

MAKING DIP STICK

An essential in using a microzoo is a well slide, which is a glass slide with a well in or on it. Well slides can be bought. One kind has the well ground into it. The other has a thin circle of glass cemented to the surface. Both kinds work well.

To make a well slide, an ordinary glass slip is used and a well added. A well can be made of cardboard with a hole punched in it. Different thickness of cardboard will, of course, give different well depths. Holes of varying size can also be made. Three or four wells, depending on size, can be put on a single glass slip.

Remember that your objective lens is small, so keep the hole for the well small. Cut the cardboard so that it fits onto the slip with no overhang.

Unless the cardboard is waterproofed, it will absorb the water from the well. It can be dipped

in shellac or varnish, or in liquid plastic. If none
of these are handy get mother or sister to cooper-
ate and coat the card with nail polish. Clear is
best, but colors can be used in an emergency.

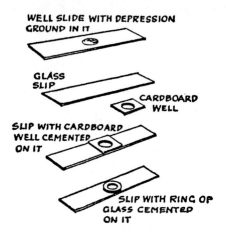

WELL SLIDE WITH DEPRESSION
GROUND IN IT

GLASS
SLIP

CARDBOARD
WELL

SLIP WITH CARDBOARD
WELL CEMENTED
ON IT

SLIP WITH RING OF
GLASS CEMENTED
ON IT

Put the card on the glass while the finish is still
wet. It will stick when it dries.

To use a well slide, dip up a specimen with
eyedropper or dip tube. With the latter, release
your thumb to suck up the specimen, then clamp
down again. The water will stay in the tube until
you release your thumb. Once the water is in the
well, put a cover slip over it, put the slide on
your microscope stage, and focus.

Always focus by setting the lens as close to the
slide as possible before applying your eye to the
ocular. Then focus by turning the control upwards. Otherwise, you're apt to fracture the cover
slip with the lens, damaging the lens at the same
time. This is particularly true with high-power
lenses.

Many specimens can be examined better if they are stained. Stain may kill the animals in some cases, so examine without stain first, then add a drop. You needn't worry about depleting the microzoo, unless you've captured only one or two of a kind. With most microscopic animals the presence of one means several dozen.

The standard stain is called methylene blue, but you may find it hard to get. An excellent substitute is Easter egg dye, which will not kill many of the animals. This dye comes in liquid, powder and paper form. Since there is a lot of variation in strength, experiment by using a concentrated solution first, then watering it a little at a time. The paper kind must be soaked in water to extract the dye. Use only a little water in a saucer, or a jar cover.

Blue fountain pen ink can also be used. But both the ink and the Easter egg dye must be strained before using. Filter paper, which can be obtained at a drug store, is best. A wad of cotton batting is next best.

Experiment with various colors. Bacteriologists use several.

You could also make a good science project by experimenting with all kinds of dyes found in the household. There are food colors, water colors used in painting, pigments to be added to paints. Try dyes soluble in solvents other than water, including mineral oil, turpentine and alcohol.

Such a project could be titled, EMPIRICAL DETERMINATION OF THE EFFICACY OF COMMON

Dyes in Staining Microorganisms. You'll find "empirical" in your dictionary. It's a good word to add to your vocabulary if you don't happen to know it.

One more stain might be mentioned. It is used specifically in staining blood samples. Next time you visit a clinic or hospital, see if you can wheedle a bit of *Wright's stain* from the technician, and ask how slides for blood examination are prepared.

You will also need alcohol. Rubbing alcohol is fine, and most houses have it. Specimens are dried by alcohol. The books mentioned at the end of the chapter will tell you how.

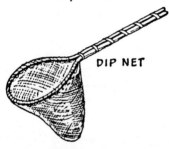

DIP NET

A dip net is the final item of equipment. Cut a length of wire about 18-inches long. A coat hanger will provide stiff wire if nothing else is at hand. Bend the wire in the middle, to make a loop, with the unused portion extending to form a double handle. Tape the two wires that form the handle, or whip them with cord, as shown in Chapter II.

A nylon stocking can be used for the net. A run in a stocking ruins it for wearing, but you don't care about appearance. Cut the stocking off between the heel and toe, and stretch the toe part over the ring you've made, sewing it in place with a few stitches.

Now, you may be in the position of a fully equipped big game hunter, but no game in sight. Perhaps it's winter and you can't rush out to collect big game the day the microscope arrives. You've studied the slides that came with the microscope until you've exhausted their possibilities. You want action!

Head for an aquarium supply store and get two things: a package of *infusoria* tablets and a bottle of brine shrimp eggs. If possible, do this in partnership with other microfans, because the smallest amount you can buy is still too much for one person to use. The tablets will cost about a quarter, and the eggs about forty cents. Prices vary from store to store and city to city.

Now you need some pure water. There is a difference between *pure* water, and *potable* water—which means water fit to drink. In most cities it is made fit to drink by the addition of chlorine that kills bacteria. Chlorine will also kill your microanimals.

Rain water is pure. So is melted snow. Distilled water can be used. Water from an aquarium is excellent. None of these at hand? Then draw tap water as hot as it comes from the heater and let it stand until cool, preferably overnight.

Drop one infusoria tablet into a pint of water. Use one of your wide-mouth jars. Leave the jar uncovered, indoors. Forget it for a couple of days.

Follow the directions on the bottle of brine

shrimp eggs to make a salt solution. Common table salt works. Sea salt or aquarium salt is somewhat better if you happen to have it, but don't buy it for the purpose.

Use only a small pinch of eggs. Drop them in the brine. The shrimp will hatch in about a day, depending on temperature. While you're waiting, examine the eggs under your microscope. If you have a fine needle try dissecting one.

When the shrimp hatch you can collect them by putting a light at one end of the jar. They will swim to the light because of phototropism—the same irresistible attraction that makes bugs come to lights and makes moths commit suicide in night fires.

The infusoria culture will develop a mob of microscopic creatures. If you hold the culture up to a light you may be able to see tiny motes in rapid motion. A drop of culture in your well slide will show you a swarm of critters, mostly paramecia, all in rapid motion.

Proper light is necessary, and too much light is about as bad as too little. A ten-watt bulb gives plenty of light for microscopy. If your microscope does not have a substage light source, which is simply a bulb in a fitting under the stage, you may want to make a box like the one shown in the illustration.

These two sources of specimens can provide hours of study and amusement. But of course there will come a time when variety becomes the spice of microscopy. This is the time to start collecting your microzoo.

A quiet pond may harbor a variety of animals and plants. If it doesn't, some other pond will. Take your net and jars with you.

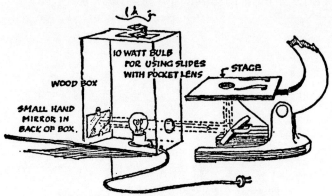

LIGHT FROM BOX REFLECTS ON MIRROR OF MICROSCOPE

Look for a trace of floating green slime. It isn't slime, but it looks like it. Your lens will show you that it's hairlike algae, and that it probably is home for several kinds of monsters. Don't take the slime out of the water: put the jar under it and float it in, water and all.

Use your net on swimming insects; they're worthy of examination, too.

A bit of waterlogged wood should go into a jar, too. Capture it underwater.

A floating leaf that may have been in the pond for a few days may also yield animals.

Watch for underwater traces of jelly or slime. Poke a little into a jar.

When your containers are full, you are in the position of the big game hunter who is in game territory, but hasn't yet seen a lion. Take your containers home and start hunting. Use your pocket lens first, and see if there are moving specks. If so, capture them with dip tube and take a look through the microscope.

One field trip will provide material for days of hunting. As you find animals, put them into separate jars of clean water—pure water, of course. Label as you identify. You'll find that manipulating a dip tube in a well slide takes more patience than fishing, a steadier hand than elephant shooting, and an iron determination. But with practice, you'll get skillful.

Besides the living specimens, you'll want specimen slides, stained and labeled, to put in your micromuseum. Sometimes you'll have only the prepared slide to show, because cultures have a mysterious way of suddenly becoming extinct—or you may find one species completely gone and another in its place. Solving such mysteries as these is fun.

To learn more of the details of owning and operating a microzoo, identifying specimens, making slides, and the host of other things that add fun to microscopy, consult your librarian. There are excellent books for beginners and advanced students. A useful and inexpensive handbook is *Hunting with the Microscope,* published by Sentinel Books for one dollar.

If you live in an area where there are no optical shops, magazines like *Science World, Science Digest, Scientific American,* and *Science News Letter* carry ads that will give you a long list of companies to which to write.

But, one word of warning: don't start unless you're prepared to go on. Exploring the microworld is the kind of hobby that doesn't let go. You'll end up boring your none-microfan friends with details of your discoveries. But you'll have a wonderful time learning more about the incredible world in which we live—and so often take for granted.

Chapter V

Your Personal Radio—Unpowered

"What we need is a radio that doesn't depend on power," Jan Miller said. "Then it would always be ready."

"I saw an old transformer in the woodshed," Rick said suddenly. "May I have it, Dr. Miller? . . . then, if I can have an old razor blade and your permission to take the receiver off the telephone for a while, I can make a radio."

The scientist, the girls and Scotty looked at him with disbelief. "He's gone off his rocker at last," Scotty muttered. "How can anyone make a radio out of junk?"

from THE BLUE GHOST MYSTERY
Chapter IX, *The Splitting Atoms.*

TO ECHO a very skeptical Scotty, how can anyone make a radio out of junk?

The answer is very easily—if the right kind of junk is at hand. Rick also needed a cardboard tube, a pencil stub, a safety pin, a few screws and a dry piece of board.

To understand how this strange assortment of odds and ends was turned into a radio, it is also necessary to have some understanding of how radio works. It's unfortunate that the theory Scotty once described won't do for the purpose.

This famous theory grew out of a question that

Barby Brant, Rick's sister, asked: "How does radio work, anyway?"

Scotty answered. "Let's imagine that we have a very long dog. In fact, this dog is so long that his tail is in New York and his nose in San Francisco. So, you step on his tail in New York and he barks in California. Radio is the same—only without the dog."

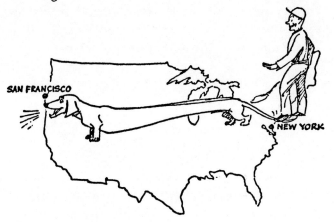

This is known as the Scotty Dog Theory of Radio Transmission.

On a slightly higher technical level, let's see what happens without the dog.

A radio transmitter is the starting point. The purpose of the transmitter is to send a continuous stream of electromagnetic waves from its antenna to the ground. Of course these waves travel through the air on their way to the ground.

The transmitter's waves are of a single, definite frequency. To understand frequency, we need an idea of what alternating electric current is. In an alternating current the electricity flows along a wire in one direction, then shifts and goes in the opposite direction. To put it in different terms, the current goes from positive to negative to positive to negative to positive . . . but you get the idea. It reverses direction in a regular pattern.

In the diagram, the line represents zero, or no flow. Starting at zero, the current rises to its highest positive point, then returns to zero. It then goes to its lowest negative point and returns to zero once again. When the current is charted, as in the diagram, the flow forms a wave.

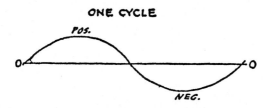

ONE CYCLE

POS.

O   O

NEG.

From zero to positive to zero to negative to zero again forms one *cycle*. Frequency is the number of times the current goes through the cycle each second. So, the definition of frequency is *cycles per second*.

You may be reading this by regular household electric light. The light is produced by an alternating current of 110 volts at a frequency of 60 cycles per second.

Electric power currents are of very low frequency, but radio frequencies are very high. Your radio is marked with dial positions numbered from 550 to 1600. Sometimes the final zero is left off, and the numbers are from 55 to 160. These numbers stand for definite frequencies.

The 55, or 550, stands for 550,000 cycles per second. The 160, or 1600, stands for 1,600,000 cycles per second. These numbers are shortened for general use by using *kilo* to mean thousand, and *meg* to mean million. So, we speak of 550 kilocycles or 1600 kilocycles. Sometimes the 1600 is shortened to 1.6 megacycles.

This range of frequencies, from 550 to 1600 kilocycles, is called the *broadcast band.* All regular radio stations, called standard broadcast stations, have a frequency within this band. They can always be found on the same position on the dial.

Since alternating currents form wave shapes, the signal sent out by the transmitter is spoken of as "radio waves." The transmitter can send its waves through the air with a signal that cannot be heard by your radio, except perhaps as a hum. This happens when the transmitter is sending only its basic, assigned frequency, called its *carrier frequency.*

Now, we leave the transmitter and go to the studio. In the studio is a microphone. Microphones are simply devices on which sound waves act mechanically. You can see an example of mechanical response to sound if you yell into a large tin can, touching the can lightly with your fingers. You'll feel it vibrate.

The microphone has parts that vibrate, too. The part may be one side of a condenser—and when it moves, the electrical capacity of the condenser is changed. The part may be a fragile ribbon of metallic foil suspended between electromagnets. When the ribbon moves, it cuts the lines of force of the magnets, and this produces an electrical current in the ribbon. Often, the microphone is a piece of crystal, of a special kind called a piezo-electric crystal. The electrical response of the crystal is changed by the pressure of sound waves on its surface.

But no matter what kind of microphone it is, it serves to change sound patterns into electrical patterns that are exact copies. If the electrical patterns were turned back into sound again they could be heard without having anything done to them to change their frequencies or other characteristics. The electrical currents from the microphone are given the name of *audio* frequencies.

The audio current leaves the microphone and is strengthened in circuits called amplifiers. The current then goes to the transmitter. The transmitter is sending out its carrier frequency. Now the audio frequency arrives and is fed right into the carrier.

This can be imagined somewhat as follows: Consider the carrier as a steady stream of water flowing in a hose. Think of the audio as a red dye fed into the hose. The dye is not a steady stream. Sometimes there's a lot—that's when the sound was loud. Sometimes there is a little—that's when the sound was soft. Sometimes there is a tiny space where there is no dye at all. That's when there was a moment of silence.

The water, now colored in streaky patterns by the dye, goes into a sprinkler that sends it in all directions—that's the carrier with the audio leaving the antenna on its way to the ground.

To use the signal created by the audio-plus-carrier, a long wire is stretched across the path of the radio waves. When you study physics, you will learn that moving a wire through the field of a magnet sets up a current in the wire. In the same way, an electromagnetic field moving across a wire also sets up a current. This is what happens: The radio waves set up a current in the wire, which, in this case, is an antenna.

To use the current set up in the antenna wire, a path must be provided through which it can travel. This path is called a circuit.

You can pick up the station you want if your circuit is *tuned*. It isn't necessary to go into the details of tuning to build the sets in this book, but it is necessary to know that tuning depends mostly on two kinds of things: *inductances* and *capacitors,* or *coils* and *condensers* as they are often called.

We have a current in the antenna and we need a circuit. The first step is a coil, an inductance, that is designed to pick up broadcast signals. The antenna wire is connected to the coil.

The radio signal we are receiving has two parts: the audio and the carrier. The carrier has done its job, by bringing the audio to us; so now we must get rid of the carrier. We do this by putting in a gate that lets the audio through but stops the carrier. Since an electrical current can't be left hanging around a gate, we provide a wire that lets it finish its voyage into the ground.

The gate that separates the audio and the carrier is called a *detector*. It detects the audio part of the signal.

From the detector we add a path through which the audio current can flow. This path is a wire that ends at one terminal of an electromagnet. From the other terminal we run a wire to ground.

As the audio current flows through the electromagnet it changes the magnetic field in a pattern that duplicates the original sound.

A very thin metal disk is held in a frame close to the magnet but not touching it. The magnet attracts the disk, and the attraction varies according to the strength of the magnetic field, which changes as the audio passes through. This causes the disk to move, as it is attracted strongly or less strongly to the magnet. The disk vibrates—and the vibrations are in the same pattern as the audio current. The vibrations of the disk form a sound pattern that can be heard. In other words, just as a microphone changes sound to electrical current by mechanical means, so does the electromagnet and disk combination turn electrical currents into sound.

The gadget has a name, of course. It is an *earphone*. Some kinds of earphone can be used as microphones, too, by reversing the procedure.

And this, in brief and oversimplified form, is how radio works. You are probably convinced by now that Scotty's Dog Theory has lots in its favor, but this explanation will help to build a radio receiver.

In the BLUE GHOST MYSTERY, Rick Brant needed to hear a weather forecast. Power and phones were out because of a storm, so Rick made an unpowered radio from junk. If we follow the construction a step at a time, you can make one, too—and see how a circuit works besides.

STEPS IN MAKING A RADIO
FROM ODDS AND ENDS

1. Rick used an old transformer that he found in the shed as a source of wire. Transformer coils are wound with yards of wire and it was his only source. You can use doorbell wire or any other thin wire you can find. It must be thin so that you can wind it into a coil. Or, you can buy wire from a radio supply store. Bare wire will do for antenna or ground, but wire for the coil should be either enameled or insulated. Wire for making connections should also be insulated.

FOXHOLE RADIO
CIRCUIT DIAGRAM

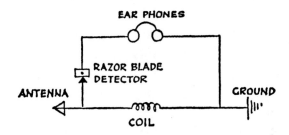

2. Rick hung about a hundred feet of wire around the room to form an antenna. This was because of stormy weather outside. You can use an outdoor antenna or one of the indoor models described later.

3. Jan Miller found a cardboard tube that had held paper toweling. Rick cut off six inches of it for use in winding his coil. Cardboard tubes from household aluminum foil or Christmas wrapping paper will do just as well. It's even simpler to use the core from a roll of toilet tissue. Rick punched two small holes at each end of the tube. He threaded one end of his insulated wire through the pair of holes at one end, leaving enough wire dangling to make a connection. The holes held the wire in place. He then wound wire tightly around the tube, keeping the turns neat and tight together. This is most easily done if one person winds while another feeds wire, keeping it tight. When the core was full of wire, Rick passed the end through the other pair of holes. This was his inductance. It would not supply accurate tuning, but it would at least enable him to hear the broadcast band, or a part of it. If you have trouble with the coil getting loose or unwinding, secure the wire with a piece of tape.

4. A piece of dry board from the shed served as a base. Rick used thumbtacks to hold the coil in place. You can use clean, shiny woodscrews. Scrape off the insulation from the dangling ends of wire and wrap them around the screws—one end to each screw. The screws will make better connections for your circuit than by twisting wires together. If you have clean washers of the right size, put one washer under each screw to help hold the wires. Don't tighten the screws yet. You have more to connect.

5. A portion of the water pipe nearest the set was scraped clean and shiny with a jackknife. (Rick also could have used a steam radiator or any of the other grounds which will be described later.) Rick connected one end of the ground wire to one end of the coil. He then ran the wire to the pipe and wrapped it tightly. Of course his connections were made with clean, bare wire. Ground connections must be clean and tight. You wind one end of your ground wire around the screw at one end of the coil, but don't tighten the screw yet.

6. Rick connected his antenna wire to the other end of the coil. You will do this by wrapping the antenna around the screw.

> *The incoming radio signal, created in the antenna, can now travel from the antenna through the coil to the ground.*

7. Rick next put a used razor blade into the circuit. It happened to be a double-edged blade. It could have been single-edged, either of white steel or blue steel. Rick used a screw to hold it to his board, close to the coil. Rick used a short length of insulated wire to connect the screw holding the razor blade to the antenna end of the coil. If you use screws at the coil ends, wrap the connecting wire right around the screw with the antenna and coil wires and screw it down tightly.

8. Jan found a pencil stub and a large safety pin. Rick broke the pencil stub off to a length of

about one inch. He bent the safety pin so that its head would lay flat on the board, as shown in the illustration. Then he pushed the sharp end into the broken end of the pencil, being sure that the pin went into the graphite lead firmly. Rick next put the pencil-pin arrangement on the board so that the sharpened end of the pencil could be moved around on the razor blade; then he used a screw to hold the head of the pin to the board. He connected a length of insulated wire to the screw and tightened it.

The incoming signal can now travel from the antenna into the coil to ground, but it will also be able to travel into the razor blade, and from the blade into the pencil, the pin, and the connecting wire. This path cannot yet be used, however, until it is connected to something.

9. Rick now connected a length of wire to the ground side of the coil. You can do the same; tighten the screw. The screw now holds the coil wire, the ground wire, and the new connecting wire.

10. With Dr. Miller's permission, since it was an emergency, Rick unscrewed the bottom plate on the telephone instrument and disconnected the pick up part of the phone. He then determined which two wires connected to the telephone's receiver part and attached them to his two loose radio wires. This completed the set, since the audio current could now travel through the razor blade-

pencil-pin combination into the electromagnet in the telephone receiver and from there into ground.

Rick may be excused for using the telephone receiver on the grounds of emergency and because he had a famous scientist to supervise him. But even so, the phone company could have made trouble had it chosen to do so. Don't try it. An earphone is better anyway, and much easier to use and connect.

To use the radio, Rick held the receiver to his ear with one hand while he carefully moved the pencil point around on the razor blade with the other. When he heard a program, he let the pencil stay in place and settled back to listen.

The whole secret, of course, is in the ability of the razor blade to act as a detector. The strange thing is that it actually works. At least it seems strange, although there is an explanation. The coating on the razor blade, which is an oxide, has the same kind of sensitive spots found in galena crystals. These spots will let direct current (the audio) pass, while blocking out the alternating carrier current. It is this selection that allows our odd little set to bring in a radio program.

The set does not work really well, because it isn't efficiently designed or properly tuned. It is not selective. It may pick up several stations at once in city areas. But such a set is as close to a basic circuit as one can get.

This kind of receiver has a name. It is known as a Foxhole radio, because it was first used by soldiers and Marines who had no other kind. Wire is common on battlefields, and yards of it can be obtained from wrecked electronic equipment. There is usually a razor blade and a pencil stub around. Coils can be wound on toilet paper cores, toothpaste boxes (a coil needn't be round) or even a piece of dry wood. Earphones come from wrecked tanks, planes or other equipment. A bayonet stuck into the ground is as good as a water pipe for a ground.

With such receivers, using only stuff common on a battlefield, a soldier could hear music and forget the war for a little while.

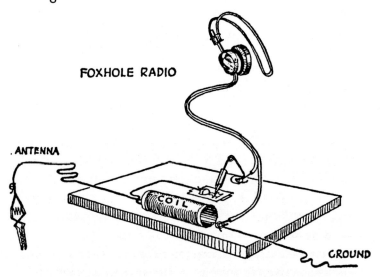

The Foxhole radio is a very primitive version of a standard receiver circuit that was commonly used when radio broadcasting first became popular. The circuits were known as crystal sets, because they used a crystal of galena as a detector. A fine, stiff wire known as a *cat whisker* was used to locate a sensitive spot on the crystal. Some radio fans still make crystal sets, experimenting with improved inductances and capacitors. The sets are used for DXing, pronounced dee-ex-ing, which is amateur (Ham) radio language for tuning in distant stations.

All crystal sets have this in common: They are unpowered, depending only on the current set up in the antenna by the incoming radio signal. This is true of commercial models that are advertised as self-powered, lifetime personal radios.

The principle differences between a Foxhole radio and a simple crystal set are these: The crystal set has a properly designed coil, with a means of changing the coil's inductance. It has a more efficient detector. It may have a condenser in the circuit to aid tuning.

There are crystal set kits on the market. One is an Official Boy Scouts of America kit, or Cub Scout kit. Some kits need only a screwdriver and a pair of pliers for assembly. Others call for a mounting board but contain everything else.

In Ham language, by the way, the board is called a breadboard. Most bread comes sliced nowadays, but when radio was young, loaves had to be sliced; and nearly every home had boards on which to do the cutting. Early Hams were apt to use mother's breadboard on which to mount their sets, and the name has stuck.

Galena crystals were about the only detectors used in crystal circuits in those days. But times have changed, and *diodes* are now used by all but a few die-hards. The diode is a highly efficient and foolproof little device that lasts practically forever. The cost is not much more than that of a crystal. Besides, diodes need no probing with a cat whisker—they detect audio without help.

One device still used in crystal and other sets is the *Fahnestock clip*. This is a spring clip in which the wire is held under tension, giving good electrical contact. These clips come in various sizes, in both double and single models. The larger ones are easier to use. If you can't get Fahnestock clips, screws will serve if clean.

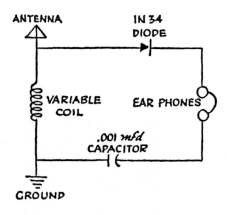

CRYSTAL RADIO CIRCUIT DIAGRAM

STEPS IN MAKING A CRYSTAL SET

Some people like to assemble kits, while others prefer to start from scratch. The advantage in making all the parts is that you will fully understand the workings of your set. The main disadvantage is slightly greater risk that the first set you build will not work well.

Start with a proper collection of parts. This is the list:

1 coil form. A toilet paper core will do.

1 strip of brass, copper or aluminum about five inches long and a half inch wide.

75 feet of #20 enameled copper wire.

1 diode, number 1N34, 1N36, or equivalent.

1 condenser, mica, .001 mfd.

1 earphone or pair of earphones, magnetic type, with a rating of over 1,000 ohms.

7 medium Fahnestock clips, or 2 double and 3 singles.

10 #4 wood screws, round head, brass or steel.

A few feet of insulated wire for connections. Bell wire or hookup wire will do.

Antenna and ground, as described later.

A mounting board. Any clean, dry 4 x 6-inch piece of wood.

If you have trouble getting any of the parts that must be purchased, talk to your radio dealer. Tell him what you want to build. He can help you choose substitutes that will work.

Collect your tools in advance, too. You will need:

A hammer.

A nail.

A screwdriver.

A knife (for removing insulation).

A piece of sandpaper.

You will find use for:

A pair of side-cutting pliers.

A gimlet or an awl for starting holes.

A pair of needlenose pliers.

Now, follow these steps.

1. Prepare the base and the coil form. Sand the base to remove splinters and to make it look neat. Then, paint both base and coil form with shellac, clear plastic paint, or varnish.

2. Wind your coil around the coil form. You can anchor the ends through holes punched with nail, awl, gimlet or knife. Or, you can secure the ends with paper fasteners if you have them. Leave a few inches of wire at each end for connecting up. Wind carefully, so that each coil of wire touches the ones next to it. Wind tightly. Put on at least 120 turns.

3. Make a slider out of your brass or metal strip. Cut a point at one end and bend it over as shown in the illustration. This is to provide a point of contact between the slider and a single strand of coil wire.

When you have a good point, drive a hole through the other end of the strip. Then bend the strip, as shown in the illustration. Place the strip so that the point will touch the wires on the coil when you move it back and forth. The strip should make contact throughout its swing across the coil. When you have it properly placed, mark the location of the end that fastens to the board. Put a screw through a clip; then screw the slider to the board.

Check the slider's swing. It should make good contact. Mark the arc where the point touches the wires, then sand off the enamel on the coil wires so the point can touch bare copper throughout its swing. Wrap a bit of tape around the slider to make a finger grip. If your fingers touch bare metal, they will affect your tuning.

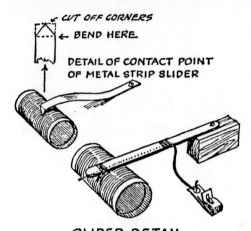

CUT OFF CORNERS

← BEND HERE.

DETAIL OF CONTACT POINT OF METAL STRIP SLIDER

SLIDER DETAIL

ALTERNATE SLIDER DESIGN USES POPSICLE STICK PIVOTED ON WOOD BLOCK. BARE WIRE ALONG BOTTOM CONTACTS COIL WIRE

4. Mount two double clips to the board as shown. If you have no doubles, put two singles on one screw.

5. You will find that your diode comes with two built-in leads. It also has a marking that will show the cathode end. Read the instructions that come with it, or the wrapping may show the marking. The cathode end goes into one of the double clips. The opposite end (the anode) goes into the clip at the antenna end of the coil.

6. The condenser also has built-in leads. Connect one to the clip at the ground end of your coil. The other lead is connected to double clip you have not yet used. From this double clip run a short wire to the slider clip.

7. Your earphones connect to the free ends of the double clips.

8. The crystal set is now ready to operate except for connecting it to antenna and ground. The ground wire goes into the clip at the ground end of the coil. The antenna wire goes into the antenna end clip.

To use the set, simply put on the earphone and listen. If you do not hear a radio signal, move the slider back and forth along the coil. Move it slowly.

If you have no success reconnect the ground to the clip on the slider and try again.

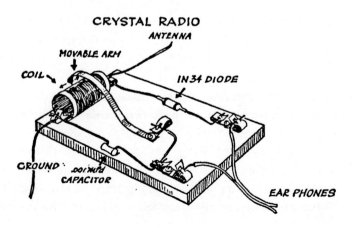

CRYSTAL RADIO

ANTENNA

MOVABLE ARM

COIL

IN 34 DIODE

GROUND

.001 MFD CAPACITOR

EAR PHONES

Still no signal? Remove the condenser and replace it with a length of hookup wire.

If there is still no signal, recheck all connections. Be especially sure that you have a good ground. Check also to be sure that your antenna and its lead wire are not making contact anywhere except at the set.

You should now be able to pick up one or more stations, depending on where you live.

Inability to pick up a program usually means poor connections somewhere in the set, a faulty earphone or the wrong kind, or a bad location. You may have to try elsewhere in the house, or even in a friend's house under some unusual conditions. There are such things as "radio shadows" caused by absorption of the signal by ground features, such as hills or mountains, by buildings with lots of steel in them, and so on. But this is a proven circuit. With good connections, a good ground and antenna, it will work anywhere a good signal is received.

MAKING A GROUND CONNECTION

A good ground is essential to the operation of the receivers discussed in this chapter and the next. This may seem strange if you are used to modern receivers without visible antenna or ground, but the designs a beginner can make require both.

This is also true of the small diode sets on the market. They are sold in the form of rockets, satellites, wrist watches, or in ordinary receiver shapes. Such sets have spring clips for connecting to an-

tenna or ground. Some have fishpole antennas
with a single clip for ground. Sometimes putting
the clip on the finger stop of a telephone is suggested. This gives you the whole telephone company for a ground or antenna.

The best ground is a good connection to a cold-
water pipe. A hot-water pipe can be used, too, but
never connect to a gas or fuel line if your workshop happens to be near them in the basement.

Pipe clamps are made for grounding appliances
to the cold-water pipes. If you have an automatic
washer or dryer at your house look for the clamp
that grounds them to the nearest pipe. Your hardware store or your appliance dealer carry such
clamps.

Next best is to wrap your ground wire around
a screw somewhere in the water system. A screw
holding a faucet handle may be the kind you can
reach easily.

If you want to use the set in your room, far
from the nearest water pipe, try the house heating system. A steam radiator makes an excellent
ground. If you have a hot air furnace there will be
radiator grilles. The screws that hold them usually go into the metal of the air ducts.

The remaining solution is to drive a pipe into
the ground under your window. Run an insulated
wire in through the window. Few windows fit so
tightly that a wire won't fit under the casement or
frame. You can also buy flat lead-ins made just for
the purpose—or you can use a small section of TV
antenna lead with the two wires twisted together
at the ends.

If you want the ground wire to be removable, equip the end with a spring clip.

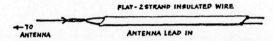

All ground connections must be clean, with bare metal to metal contact. The shorter your ground wire is, the better—and remember, the set is only as good as your ground.

MAKING AN ANTENNA

The best antenna is a long, high wire out of doors. It should be from 50 to 100 feet in length, and placed high above the ground. This is seldom possible except in suburban or rural areas. But if you do have space, here is how the antenna is made:

Use copper strand antenna wire. The antenna and lead-in to the house should be one continuous length. The wire must be insulated at both ends, at the points where it is attached to the supports. Glass or ceramic insulators can be purchased. You can make your own insulators, too. Dry wood is an excellent insulator if it is really dry and can be kept that way. Any small pieces of wood can be used. Bake in a warm oven to get the moisture out, then drill two holes or use screweyes. Then waterproof the wood with any good paint, plastic, varnish or shellac. Let dry between coats, and give extra coats as needed to the ends that absorb the most paint. Use as shown in the illustration.

The antenna lead-in should enter the house by

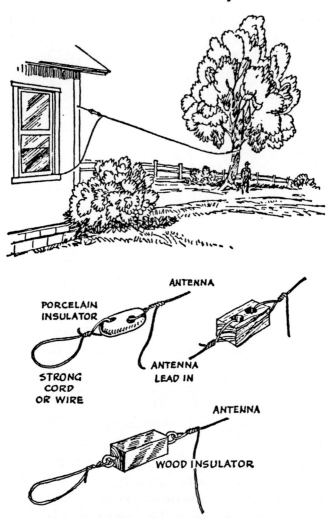

way of a flat copper lead-in strip, which is properly insulated, or you may use TV lead wire.

Be careful not to hang your antenna over or under other wires. Avoid power or telephone poles as supports. Trees that sway in the wind should be

avoided, too. Try to keep the antenna away from
house metal, such as gutters. Every outdoor antenna should have a lightning arrester on it.
These can be purchased.

If you live in a neighborhood where an outdoor
antenna is not possible, or if you want your set to
be completely portable, there are two good indoor rigs you can make.

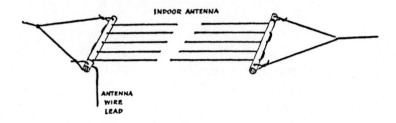

The first is made from a coil of bell wire, or
from about 60 feet of regular copper strand antenna wire. Two pieces of wood about seven
inches long are needed, and some means of drill-
ing holes. The illustration shows how the antenna
is assembled.

The second indoor antenna is made of the kind
of flat spring toy that "walks" downstairs. The toy
is often called a "slinky," although that is just one
name. A piece of insulated wire or heavy cord is
tied around the last two coils on each end. The
spring can then be stretched across the room and
the ends tied to convenient projections, like dra-
pery rods, the top hinge on a door, and so on. If
straightened out, the coil would be a long, flat
piece of steel. Since it is in coil form, you get the
same usable length in a small space. Further-

more, the coil has the same useful properties as the coil in your set—it has inductance.

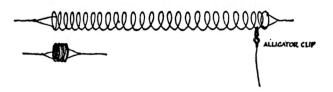

INDOOR "SLINKY" ANTENNA

ALLIGATOR CLIP

To connect your lead wire to the coil use an alligator clip. Scrape the finish from a section near one end and attach the clip.

The spring antenna is completely portable, easy to handle, and not expensive.

One more tip. If you get into a situation where one connection is missing, substitute your own body by pressing a moist finger on the connection. For instance, if you have an antenna but no ground, your body will act as a "counterpoise antenna" and may help bring in a station. Your body inductance may be useful in improving a signal, too, even with antenna and ground. Touch finger to ground or antenna and see for yourself.

COMMENTS ON CRYSTAL SETS

It would be easy to fill an entire book with information on crystal sets. They are simple, but far from being out of style. One thing is fairly certain, however; you won't be satisfied with the first one you make. This is because it is not selective—which means that you can't separate stations—and it is not very powerful.

The crystal set does have one major advantage, though. It needs no power. Knowing how to make one may come in handy some day, and starting with a simple set will help to understand more complicated ones.

There are many variations in crystal sets, and many ways of getting the same results. For instance, a slider can be made from a block of wood, a tongue depresser or popsicle stick, and a piece of stiff copper wire, as shown.

Crystals can be improvised, too. Fool's gold (iron pyrites) has sensitive crystals and so do other minerals. You could even make a very good science project or Boy Scout project out of experimenting with crystals and circuits as a means of receiving Civil Defense emergency instructions. Such a project could include development of coil specifications for tuning only to the emergency frequencies of 640 and 1240 kilocycles—whichever is in use in your area.

If unpowered sets interest you and you want to make a really good one, look in the classified ad sections of magazines like *Popular Mechanics, Science and Mechanix, Popular Electronics,* and so on. You will find ads for catalogues, for crystal set designs, for parts and even instructions—all in the special field of crystal sets. Alfred Morgan's fine book, *The Boy's Second Book of Radio and Electronics* also has details on better crystal circuits.

But start with the simplest and work up. It's easier that way—and the learning is painless.

Chapter VI

Your Personal Radio—With Power

Rick sighed. He waved at Barby. "Look at her. So young, so smart, so pretty. But the poor girl has a very slight handicap. She has to wear a hearing aid."

Scotty got it then. "Hey! Rick, that's great! The hearing aid would be a radio receiver!"

from THE ELECTRONIC MIND READER
Chapter I, *The Million Dollar Gimmick.*

THE INVENTION that makes possible a radio as small as a hearing aid is the marvelous transistor, the little giant of the world of electronics.

The transistor is what is known as a "solid state device." There are actually several kinds of transistors, but we are concerned with only one: the PNP Junction Transistor.

These tiny devices, scarcely larger than a full-grown pea, can replace the vacuum tube in some types of circuits. However, the transistor is not just a substitute for a tube. It can do different things, too, and it operates on an entirely different principle.

Junction transistors are made of a tiny piece of germanium. A wire, called the *emitter,* is attached to the input side of the germanium wafer through a dot of some other metal, often indium. A second wire, called the *base,* is connected to the germanium itself. A third wire, called the *collector,* is connected to the output side, again through a piece of indium.

It might be helpful to think of the emitter as a high reservoir of electrons that flow over a dam into the collector when given a little push by electrons flowing in from outside—from a battery. The dam can be raised or lowered to control the flow of electrons. This is done by feeding a few electrons into the dam, or the base, to name the proper element of the transistor.

Compared to electron tubes in their fragile glass cases, the transistor is pretty tough. But it can be damaged by a sharp blow or by excessive heat. This means, in practical terms, that it is not a good idea to drop transistors, or to drop things on them. It also means great care must be taken in soldering.

No soldering of transistors is called for in this chapter, but if you insist on trying it, it is necessary to use a pencil-type soldering iron and to wrap wet tissue around the wire being soldered. The heat of the iron is used up in heating the water in the tissue and does not reach the transistor. Of course heat can be applied directly to the solder. The idea is to prevent heat transmission up the lead wire to the germanium.

Most transistors are sold with instructions on how to tell one lead from another. However, the transistor named as first choice in this chapter does not; so be sure to consult the sketch of the transistor once you're ready to begin work.

It is the small size of transistors that has made

miniature electronic devices possible. They are used in eyeglasses hearing aids, for instance, in company with a mercury battery little larger than an aspirin tablet. You can make a very compact receiver, too, if you are skilled with a soldering iron and other radio tools. This is done by changing the positions of the parts in the transistor receiver to be described later on and by using a compact case. True miniaturization, however, depends on printed circuits as much as on transistors.

This chapter assumes that you are a true beginner in radio construction. The circuits are designed for simple construction. Anyone can make them by following the directions and studying the diagrams.

More compact designs for advanced amateurs can be found in nearly every issue of the popular electronics and radio magazines. Radio dealers have booklets issued by transistor manufacturers that give designs for all sorts of items. Some companies also sell complete kits for do-it-yourself transistor radios.

A TRANSISTORIZED AMPLIFIER

The first project is to make an amplifier using a single transistor. The amplifier can be used to increase the volume of the crystal set described in the last chapter. Or, it can be used to amplify the signal from weak stations received by the single transistor receiver to be described later.

In all projects, assemble all parts and tools first. Study the instructions and the diagrams. Be sure you know what you're going to do before you start. Then, recheck instructions and diagrams as you go.

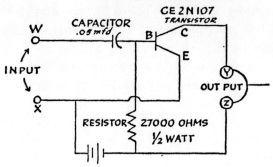

TRANSISTORIZED AMPLIFIER
CIRCUIT DIAGRAM

Parts List

1 PNP transistor, GE 2N107, or equivalent.
1 capacitor (condenser) .05 microfarads.
1 resistor, 27,000 ohms, ½ watt.
4 #2 Fahnestock clips.
10 #4 brass wood screws, round head, with copper or brass washers to match.
1 double battery holder.
2 1½-volt batteries to fit holder.
Hookup wire.
Wooden base, 4 x 5 inches, dried and varnished.

Tools

Awl or gimlet for starting holes.
Screwdriver to fit #4 screws.
Needlenose pliers.
Knife for removing insulation, if necessary.

The battery holder may be purchased, in which case a soldering job must be done to connect lead wires. This is most satisfactory. It is also possible to solder leads directly to the batteries which can then be held to the board by tape and tacks, or by a scrap of aluminum. Third best is to make a battery holder from scraps of aluminum. If a holder is made, you can use ordinary AA flashlight cells. But the small Penlite cells are neater and work just as well.

To understand the assembly of radio circuits it is necessary to know a few symbols that are used to designate parts. These symbols are standard. Getting acquainted with them will help you to see the relationships of parts in all circuits. There are many symbols used in electronics, but only those used in the circuits in this chapter are illustrated below. For others, see the books listed at the end of the chapter.

SYMBOLS USED IN CIRCUIT DIAGRAMS:

SYMBOLS USED IN CIRCUIT DIAGRAMS

Study the circuit diagram and try to figure out the relationship of the parts. If you learn the diagram well, it will be easier to make variations in the actual layout. *Note that the circuit diagram is not a plan for putting the circuit together.* It is only to help you understand what you're doing.

Next step is to check the parts of the circuit against the written instructions and the sketch showing the actual layout.

Finally, assemble tools and parts and proceed with the assembly. Keep rechecking the circuit diagram, layout sketch and instructions as you go. Work slowly and carefully.

1. Lay out the parts, not including the batteries, on the wooden base. Put the parts in the positions they will actually occupy. Move the parts around to get the most compact layout possible, still leaving room to make connections. You will use the leads built into the transistor, diode, capacitor and resistor; so your layout must be compact enough to allow these leads to reach the connections. When you are satisfied that the layout is as good as you can make it, use a pencil to mark the places where the screws will go.

2. Make your screw holes and start the screws. The awl or gimlet will help you. Where terminals are needed, put Fahnestock clips on the screws, using a single washer between the clip and the screwhead. You will wrap the connecting wires and leads under the washers later. Where simple screw connections are indicated, use a screw and two washers. The wires will be held between the

washers. (The washers are not essential; but with them the wire has less chance of slipping out when you tighten the screw.)

3. Anchor the battery box down. Do not insert the batteries just yet.

4. Wrap one lead wire from the capacitor around the screw holding input Fahnestock clip W. Wrap the other lead around connecting screw B.

5. Wrap one lead wire from the resistor around screw B. Connect the other end of the resistor to the negative (−) terminal of the battery. Or you can wrap it around the screw holding output Fahnestock clip Z.

6. If you are using a commercial battery holder, it will be necessary to solder lead wires to the battery terminals. When ready, connect the hookup wire from the negative (−) side of your battery holder to Fahnestock clip Z.

7. Use a length of hookup wire to connect the screw holding input Fahnestock clip X to the positive (+) battery terminal. Then connect a lead wire from the (+) terminal to E.

8. You are now ready for the transistor. Recheck the instructions to be sure you know which lead is which. Spacing for identification of leads on a GE 2N107 is shown on page 137. The emitter lead goes to connection E. The base lead goes to con-

nection B. And the collector lead goes to C, which is then connected by a short length of wire to the screw holding output Fahnestock clip Y.

9. Recheck and tighten all connections. The amplifier is finished and you can now add batteries. Snap them into the holder, being sure they point the right direction. If in doubt, mark your base at each end of the holder to remind you of how the batteries go in. The negative end of the battery is the smooth, flat one. The positive end has the circular terminal sticking out. To get three volts, the batteries must be in series.

A TRANSISTORIZED
AMPLIFIER

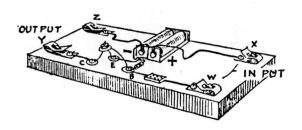

Now, to use your amplifier, put pieces of hookup wire into the input terminals. Connect these wires to the terminals on the crystal set where you normally plug in your earphones. The earphones are connected to the output terminals on the amplifier.

Tune in your station. Louder? Yes, as amplified by a one transistor audio amplifier. Congratulations!

A ONE-TRANSISTOR RECEIVER

This receiver is designed for a breadboard layout, because that's the easiest kind to make. When you've assembled it and have had some fun with it, you can try reassembling it to fit into a case. With very little change, except for squeezing the parts a little closer together, this set will fit into two common types of plastic box. One is the kind in which assortments of screws are packaged. It is a hinged box of clear plastic, measuring about 5 and ¾ inches long, 3 and ¼ inches wide, and 1 and ¼ inches high. The other box is the kind in which two spools of good fishing line come packed. It measures 5¾ x 2⅞ x 1½, and has oval ends. The cover is fitted, but not hinged.

If you decide to use either of these boxes, put your set base in the cover. Make the base from quarter-inch plywood. Drill holes for the variable capacitor and loopstick, but be careful because the plastic cracks easily. Smaller holes will be needed for antenna and ground wires, and for earphone connections.

You can purchase all new parts for this receiver and use your amplifier for increasing the signal of weak stations, or you can "cannibalize" the amplifier and re-use the transistor, the diode and the clips.

Parts List

1   PNP transistor, GE 2N107 or equivalent.
1   diode, 1N34 or equivalent.
1   capacitor, fixed, disk or equivalent, .02 microfarads.

1 capacitor, variable, tuning, flat midget type, 365 microfarads.

1 loopstick.

1 resistor, 220,000 ohms, ½ watt.

4 #2 Fahnestock clips.

14 #4 brass wood screws, round head, with washers.

2 knobs to fit loopstick and capacitor shafts.

Wooden base, 5 x 6 inches.

Hookup wire, approximately 2 feet.

Antenna and ground (see Chapter V)

Battery holder and two 1½-volt penlite batteries.

The new elements in this set are the tuning capacitor and the loopstick. Tuning a receiver depends on capacitors and inductances. The variable capacitor is a standard type that tunes the broadcast band when used with a proper inductance.

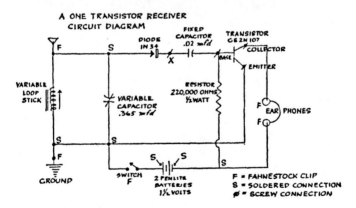

The loopstick is the inductance. It is made of very fine wire wound around a waxed cardboard tube. The winding may seem rather bumpy under its waxed covering because it is "scramble" wound. Inside the cardboard tube is a slug of metal called a ferrite slug because of the iron compound used. This slug can be moved in and out by turning the screw shaft that projects from one end. As the slug moves, the inductance of the coil is changed. This contributes to fine tuning.

Your tools will be the same as those used in making the amplifier, with one addition. Some means of soldering will be necessary. If you have no soldering iron at home and no one to show you how to solder, it's very likely that the TV or radio repairman who services your home equipment will do it for you.

Before going into the details of assembly, let's recognize a hard fact of life. It very often happens that the enthusiastic do-it-yourselfer rushes off to the dealer's, shopping list in hand, only to find that the dealer doesn't have certain items. What to do? The dealer may be unwilling to order one or two small parts, or the eager buyer may not want to wait.

The answer is to substitute something else. That's why the word equivalent is used in the parts list—because substitutes are possible. Equivalent, however, doesn't mean the same price, shape, color, or size. It means the *electrical* equivalent, something that will do the same job in a circuit. A good dealer knows equivalents. He has books from the manufacturers and other sources to help him.

Nearly everything in a circuit can be substituted in one way or another, because there are many ways of getting the same result. For instance, the number and kinds of capacitors is enormous. The value in microfarads, which is the measure of capacitance, can almost always be obtained, although the kind you want may not be available.

The specifications call for a variable capacitor of 365 mfd, flat miniature type. The dealer will almost certainly have a 365 mfd variable capacitor; but suppose it's a panel mount model, rather than a flat mount? Take it, and put a panel on your set. A panel can be made from any thin wood, like orange-crate wood, or a piece of composition board. It's only necessary to nail it to the base so it is in an upright position. Holes can then be drilled to take both the capacitor and loopstick shafts.

No special make of loopstick is required. There are many to choose from, and the dealer can find you an inexpensive one if you tell him what it is to be used for.

There are several transistors that will serve. However, if you use a different model than the one specified, you will probably need a fixed capacitor and resistor of different ratings. Ask your dealer about this.

You can buy a switch from your dealer, too, to turn off the set when not in use. Or, you can make one easily. (To make a switch, use a slightly longer wire between the positive terminal of the battery and the emitter connection. Cut it at some convenient point. Wrap one lead around a screw holding a Fahnestock clip. Insert the other lead into the clip to make the connection; take it out to disconnect. That's all there is to it.)

Here's an extra tip: Radio engineers are about the friendliest professional people in the world. If you live near a radio transmitter, drop in. Get acquainted with the engineers. If they're like most of their breed, they'll be glad to talk over your problems and show you ways of getting good results.

Now to assemble your transistor receiver. Read the instructions. Study the circuit diagram. Study the drawing. Recheck parts and tools. If you need to have soldering done by someone else, plan your work accordingly. If not, go to it.

1. Mount the variable capacitor. You may need small washers or pieces of cardboard between the bottom of the capacitor and the baseboard. This is to allow the shaft to rotate freely. It may also be possible to drill a shallow hole slightly larger in diameter than the shaft.

2. Unpack the loopstick. There is usually loose wire coiled around it. Remove this wire. You won't need it. With the loopstick will be a small strip of aluminum, the loopstick mounting bracket. Bend it carefully, to make an L-shaped mount. The metal end of the loopstick snaps into the large hole. The smaller holes are to screw it to the base. Check to see if you could use a screwdriver for mounting if the loopstick were in place. If not, screw the bracket down first, then insert the loopstick. Use care. Push gently until

the metal end snaps into place. Note that two lugs project from the loopstick on opposite sides of the tube. These are copper loops, for soldering.

3. Once the variable capacitor and loopstick are in place, you can add the Fahnestock clips for connecting ground and antenna. The clips for the earphones can now be put in place. Don't tighten the screws on your clips yet, however.

4. Put a screw in the board at point X. Use washers on the screw if you have them. This will be the tie point for your diode and one lead of the fixed capacitor. Add other screws at points E, B, and C. These will be the tie points for the three leads from your transistor.

5. Mount the battery box next. As you locate it on the board, keep the circuit in mind. Leads will run from the positive terminal (+) to the loopstick and to the emitter. The resistor will be connected between the negative terminal (−) and the base tie point. (The fixed capacitor also will tie in at B.)

If you want a switch or a Fahnestock clip battery connection, now is the time to put it in place.

6. Put knobs on the variable capacitor and loopstick shafts. If the dealer doesn't have knobs, take time to make some. Remember, knobs need not be round. Put a hole of the proper size through a wafer of wood, perhaps a piece from a popsicle stick. Hold your makeshift knobs in

place with glazier's points, bits of toothpick, or
slivers of wood. If there is plastic aluminum in the
house, it will lock the knobs on permanently.

A ONE TRANSISTOR RECEIVER

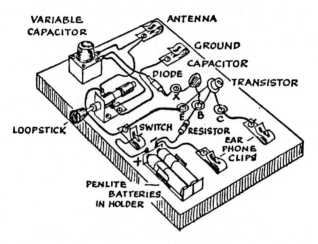

7. The receiver is now assembled and only the
wiring remains. Remember, the transistor goes
into place last.

Before you begin wiring, here's a point to consider. All sets in this book are based on ease of assembly. This receiver needs soldering, but at
only a few points. It is even possible to avoid
soldering if you hold the lead wires in place on
the soldering lugs with a metallic glue or plastic
metal. Soldering, however, gives the best results.
Many builders either will be able to solder, or
they will have a relative or friend who can do it
for them. For such lucky folks, keep this in mind:
Any connection is improved by soldering, includ-

ing connections for the Foxhole radio and the crystal set. If you can, solder everything but the transistor leads. This can be done by using tie points, which are tiny bits of metal with a hole for a screw in one end and a very small hole to take a piece of bare hookup wire in the other. The wire is passed through, bent over and then soldered.

Tie points may be used at all connections that are on the base. When used at the Fahnestock clips, the tie point is held by the screw that holds the clip. Once the screw is tightened down, a drop of solder will connect it better to the brass of the clip.

If you are sure of yourself, you can even solder the transistor leads, but be sure to keep the heat from running up the wire by using a piece of wet tissue. Do this in soldering the diode, too.

1. The loopstick. Facing the knob, solder two hookup wires to the right-hand lug. Solder the loose end of one of these pieces to the lug on the corner of the variable capacitor. The other piece goes to the antenna clip. Still facing the knob, solder two pieces to the left-hand lug. One piece goes to the ground clip. The other piece goes to the battery holder's positive (+) terminal.

2. The battery holder. This may have insulated connectors at both ends. You can tell easily enough because the insulation looks like a tiny cardboard disk. Solder a bare piece of wire between the connectors at one end. This is so the two batteries can

be placed in series. If the holder has insulated terminals at only one end, this step is unnecessary.

Solder to the positive (+) terminal the length from the loopstick and a piece long enough to reach E. Strip off a half inch of insulation from the second wire and wrap the bare wire around the E screw. (Of course, you use bare wire at all connections.)

To the negative (−) terminal solder a piece of hookup wire and one lead from the resistor. The other resistor lead goes to connection B. The wire goes to the nearest earphone connecting clip.

3. The variable capacitor. It has two soldering lugs. One is in the middle of a side, the other near a corner. To the middle lug, solder a piece of wire. The other end goes to the ground clip. To the corner lug solder the wire from the right-hand lug of the loopstick. To this corner you must now solder the proper lead from the diode. Protect it from heat if you can.

The diode has two leads, and the one for you to identify comes out of the *cathode* end. The other end, the anode, is seldom marked. In fact, there is sometimes difficulty in being sure about the cathode. If the diode is one of the types that looks like a tiny plastic bottle, it may have the diode symbol stamped on plastic. In this symbol (see page 124) the arrow points to the cathode. Or, one shoulder of the plastic bottle may be painted. If in doubt, get a magnifying glass. It is a good idea to check with the dealer at the time of purchase, too. Other types of diode may be clear or opaque plastic cylinders. These usually have a stripe around them at the cathode end.

Once you've identified the cathode end, solder the *opposite* end to the corner lug of the variable capacitor. In other words, your cathode should be pointing away from the capacitor lug. The cathode end may now be connected to the screw connection marked X. It will share this connection with one lead of the fixed capacitor.

4. Connect the fixed capacitor to the screw at point X. Connect the other lead to connection B.

5. Use a piece of hookup wire to connect the unused earphone clip to connection C.

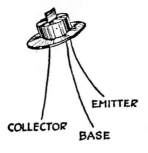

TRANSISTOR

EMITTER

COLLECTOR   BASE

6. Locate the proper leads on your transistor. Recheck the instructions that came with it, even if you think you're sure. Unfortunately, some transistors do not come with clear instructions, and one of them may be the 2N107. If you're using one of these, the spacing will make it easy. Notice

that two leads are close together, with one a little distance away at the other side of the transistor bottom. The outside one of the close pair is the emitter. The inside one of the pair is the base. The collector is the lead that is off by itself.

Connect these leads to the screw at points E, B, and C. As in all connections, your needlenose pliers will make it easy to form loops that go around the screws. If you don't have the proper pliers, use your fingers.

7. Recheck all connections. Tighten down all screws. Put your batteries in the holder. One goes in with its flat end toward the negative (−) terminal, which holds the resistor lead. The other goes in with its projecting metal disk toward the positive (+) terminal.

8. Hook up antenna and ground. Connect earphones. Put on earphones and you're in business!

Now to experiment with tuning. The loopstick shaft will have from ten to a dozen full turns in and out. The variable capacitor shaft will turn through a half circle. Turn the loopstick shaft until you hear a station; then use the variable capacitor to get maximum volume. Make small adjustments in both until the station is as clear and loud as you can make it.

See how many stations you can pick up both by night and day. By night, many more stations usually can be heard. In fact, on a clear winter's night the broadcast band may be so jammed that you can't separate one from the other.

If there is not enough volume and your amplifier hasn't been cannibalized to make the receiver, hook it up by connecting the earphone clips of the set to the input clips on the amplifier as you did for the crystal set.

Good listening! And good experimenting if you try to make a more compact set later. You may think you prefer television to radio for entertainment, as opposed to radio for experimental construction purposes, but keep this in mind: You can't take a TV set to bed with you and enjoy music after the lights are out.

Radio construction is one field in which the library can be of invaluable help to you. Consult the library's card catalogue and you'll be surprised at the number of books on the subject. Some are simple, and some are hard. You'll be able to pick the ones you want by examining them.

One excellent book for the beginner is Alfred Morgan's *The Boys' Second Book of Radio and Electronics.* It goes into very useful detail on many experimental circuits.

The *Radio Amateur's Handbook* by A. Frederick Collins has much useful information. This book is often confused with another excellent one of the same title published by the American Radio Relay League. The ARRL book is the standard in the field of amateur, or Ham, radio. It can tell you how to get a license, how to make transmitters, and so on.

There are several how-to-do magazines on radio and electronics. Most issues carry simple transistor circuits, and they contain ads. Look especially in the classified ad sections. Try *Popular Mechanics,* too. Write for the catalogues and literature that are advertised. They're fun to read, and you may be able to order parts very cheaply.

For now, CUL OM 73, which in Ham code is: See you later, old man. Best regards.

Chapter VII

The Modern Bowman

Rick fitted the arrow's nock to the bowstring, got his fingers in position to draw, and flexed the bow slightly. Then, taking a deep breath, he stepped calmly forward to the edge of rock.

It took only three steps to bring him within sight of the guard. He had a quick vision of a black velvet cap, hunched shoulders, and a rifle held casually across the knees. He drew smoothly, held for the briefest instant, and released the shaft. Scotty was at his side, rifle ready, the moment the shaft left the bow.

from THE PIRATES OF SHAN
Chapter XVIII, *Under Cover of Darkness*

YOU MAY never have a chance to take a bowshot at a pirate. But if you ever should, it would certainly be wise to be prepared. There's nothing worse than falling into the hands of pirates if you're not ready.

But seriously, pirates or not, you can get more fun out of modern archery than from most sports, if you enjoy roaming in the woods, if you get a thrill out of developing new skills and using them, and if you have a pal to shoot with.

The buddy system isn't necessary in archery, but it's always more fun doing things with someone else. Archery is no exception.

First, we have to understand the different forms of archery. There are two, of which this chapter is concerned with only one.

Field archery and *target archery* are the two names given to the different forms. The names are descriptive. The field archer roams the fields and woods, while the target archer shoots at a fixed target. A good target archer is not usually a good field archer, while the field archer cannot hope to equal the target archer on his own ground.

To see why this is so, we have to examine the flight of an arrow.

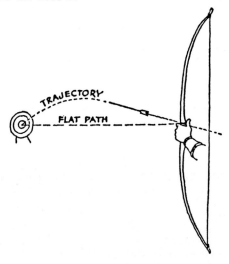

The arrow does not travel a flat path, or trajectory, except across very short distances. From the moment the arrow leaves the bow, gravity is pulling it downward. At first the velocity of the arrow keeps it moving in a flat trajectory; but the attraction of gravity soon starts it curving down, with a loss of velocity followed by a sharper curve, and so on until the arrow hits the ground. To put it another way, the farther the arrow travels the more velocity it loses, and the more velocity it loses the more sharply it curves toward the ground, as the illustration shows.

What this means is simply that the arrow does not travel in a straight line from archer to target, except across short distances. When the archer is any appreciable distance from the target, he has to shoot up in the air at more or less of an angle in order to keep the arrow airborne until the target is reached.

In addition, the archer cannot sight down the arrow as he sights down the barrel of a rifle. Or, if he does manage to sight down the length of the arrow, you can be certain he's holding bow and arrow improperly.

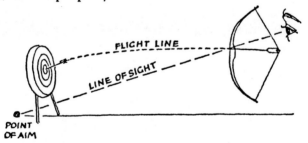

So the archer must sight indirectly, and he must allow for the arrow's curving path.

The target archer takes these two factors into account by using artificial aids. Some target archers use a sight that fastens to the bow. The sight can be set for different distances. Most target archers, however, use a "point of aim."

When the target archer is close to the target, the

point of aim is somewhere on the ground between archer and target. When the target is far away, the point of aim is somewhere beyond the target.

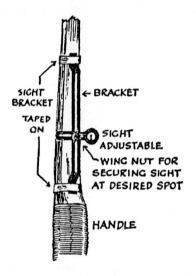

SIGHT
BRACKET

← BRACKET

TAPED
ON

SIGHT
ADJUSTABLE

WING NUT FOR
SECURING SIGHT
AT DESIRED SPOT

HANDLE

Target tournaments are always shot at the same distances, and it is at these distances that the target archer practices. For example, if you were to shoot in a tournament, you would probably shoot in the Junior American Round, Boy's Division. You would shoot 30 arrows at each distance of 30, 40, and 50 yards.

Naturally, all your practice would be at those distances. You would know your point of aim for each one.

Tournaments, and practice for them, take place under specified rules established by the American Archery Association. A standard target is used. In most cases the tournament takes place in a public park, or on a club range, where the ground is level, and the grass is green and clipped short so arrows can be easily found if they go astray.

Now, compare the activities of the target archer with those of the field archer. Robin Hood was a field archer. He hunted both the King's deer and the King's men, or at least the Sheriff of Nottingham's bullies.

Robin Hood never knew what distance would be next, whether he would be shooting uphill, downhill or on the level, whether he would be shooting across a clearing or through woods filled with branches and twigs that might deflect his arrows.

Robin had to be ready to get off a quick shot or several quick shots in any direction, at any angle, and at any distance within bowshot. He had to shoot equally well while standing, crouching, sitting or kneeling.

Bow sights or points of aim were not for Robin Hood, nor are they for today's field archer. There is no time to set a bow sight while hunting, and no time to figure out distance or proper point of aim.

Very often, when hunting, there isn't even time to think. The archer must react, properly and instantly, and *instinctively*.

The field archer is an instinctive shooter. He just shoots. He doesn't aim, at least consciously. He doesn't worry about his position; he'll shoot from under a branch, around a tree, or across the open fields.

Target archery is a contest.

Field archery is a game.

Field archery is both old and new. It was practiced by the original bowmen—whoever they were. We know this because man, back at the dawn of history when the bow was invented, was a hunter and not a sportsman. Just keeping alive and fed took all of a man's time. His bow was a tool for hunting and for war. Perhaps in later centuries, the bow also became useful to show off a man's skill and strength in what were the start of contests.

As guns grew common, the bow vanished from general use. Fortunately, it didn't vanish entirely. In Europe, die-hards who were opposed to gunpowder continued to hold up the bow as the ideal weapon for man, and the idea took hold that archery was a manly kind of thing to know. Archery purely for its own sake followed naturally, and sportsmen in England kept the bow active.

In 1828 the sport of archery came to America. The first archery club, in Philadelphia, is still in existence.

But archery had undergone the great change. It was no longer a game, no longer something a man had to know to eat and live. Archery was now a contest, and a pretty formal one at that. The purpose of archery was the tournament, with its formal rounds, its huge targets with the familiar white, blue, red and golden rings.

This is the way things stood until enough archers grew tired of the formalities, the essential artificiality of aiming points and bow sights, to start a small revolution that has grown and grown until today many men hunt the deer in the greenwood forest and many more belong to clubs specializing in field archery, bow hunting, or both.

The modern bowman is a field archer. He is a hunter, or he may become one. He plays the game of field archery in about the same way that the ardent golfer plays the game of golf. He has a good time at it, too.

Boys are encouraged to become field archers. They are encouraged to join their elders in hunting, when they are old enough and skillful enough.

There are field archery clubs in many cities and towns. In the big cities there may be several.

One sign of the increased interest in archery is the amount of equipment sold. Not many years ago it was rare to find archery equipment except in the largest sporting goods stores. Now it is found in department stores, the so-called "surplus" stores, and may be bought from mail order catalogues.

Enough people have become interested in archery to make it worth while for manufacturers to start turning out equipment by mass production methods.

One important effect of mass production is that manufacturers are never satisfied. They are constantly trying to make a product with a fewer number of production steps, with less expensive materials, of lighter weight to save shipping charges, and so on. At the same time, they must maintain or improve their quality, in order to compete with their competitors.

Very often, this effect results in a better product at a lower price. Archery has benefited in just this way.

There are now available, from several different

companies, bows made of fiberglass. They range in price from about $2.50 to ten times that much. The cheapest of these bows is, in the opinion of some experts, better than the very best bow the average person is capable of making himself.

In some parts of the country the cheapest fiberglass bow costs less than the wood from which to make a traditional wooden bow, and it is in many respects a better bow—assuming that the particular fiberglass bow in question is the product of a reputable manufacturer, and sold by a reputable store.

Naturally, the better the bow the higher the cost. This is as true in archery as in anything else, and it applies to all other equipment as well as the bow.

At the cheaper prices, the bow is apt to be simply a piece of fiberglass, properly tapered, with nocks at the ends to take the bowstring, and a piece of plastic, cloth or tape for a handle. Also, it is apt to be unrated.

The bow should have a handle. Furthermore, the handle should form an arrow rest, or the bow should have a separate arrow rest. Shooting arrows across the unprotected hand has a way of tearing gashes in the thin skin between thumb and forefinger.

The bow should be rated in pounds, and in inches of draw. For example, a very common rating for a bow such as you might buy would be 20 pounds at 26 inches. This means that it takes 20 pounds of pull to draw the bow fully with a 26-inch arrow.

But suppose your arms are shorter than this, and you can only draw a bow to 22 inches? Then you could not draw a 20-pound bow far enough to actually pull 20 pounds. Instead, you would be pulling something like 12 to 15 pounds, depending on the bow.

The power of a bow does not increase in direct proportion to the amount of draw; that is, half-drawing a 20-pound bow does not mean that the bow is pulling 10 pounds. It would take about a three-quarter draw to pull 10 pounds, or even more, depending on the individual bow.

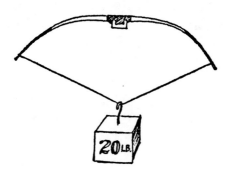

Bows produced by mass methods are usually rated in even numbers of 15, 20, 25, 30, 35, 45, 50, 55, 60 and on up to even more pounds. Hand-crafted bows, including mass produced composite bows of wood and plastic or fiberglass, may have in-between ratings like 27 pounds, 32 pounds, and so on, as well as the even numbers.

The question is: how heavy a bow should you get?

This shouldn't be a problem, but pride makes it one. It has happened that a boy—call him Joe—shows up one day and says proudly, although casually, "Hey, you smalltimers. Take a look at a real bow. Hunting weight."

You look, all right, and it is. Clearly, plainly, stamped into the handle of the bow is the magic number: 45 pounds at 28 inches. This is the minimum hunting weight in most states, whether at 26 or 28 inches makes no difference.

Joe swaggers a little. The rest of you look at him with mixed emotions, envy prominent among them. Joe nocks an arrow and shoots at the bale of hay the club uses for a target backstop, and the arrow goes in almost up to the feathers.

This is big medicine. You forget common sense. You turn the livid green of the forest primeval, with envy.

Please don't. Do not envy the mighty warrior with the big, big bow. Instead, pity him. Be kind to him when he brags about his man-size weapon. For Joe is overbowed. He doesn't know it yet, but he will, even though he'd rather die the Death Of A Thousand Cuts than admit it.

Get the gang together and go on a game of rovers. This is a simple game. You agree on a target—say that old stump at the edge of the woods for the first one. You shoot an agreed number of arrows at the stump, perhaps four. The one with the highest number of hits chooses the second target, and so on. Clumps of grass, streaks in a clay bank, logs, stumps, or anything else that's soft enough and also dead will serve for a target.

You cover a mile and massacre ten targets. At four arrows each, you have shot 40 arrows.

THE ARROW GOES IN ALMOST UP TO THE FEATHERS

Joe hasn't done very well. He started out in his usual form, which is about average, but he slowed down. He blames this on unfamiliarity with the new bow. Wait until he gets used to it, he says. You suggest another round of rovers, to help him get used to it, but he's had enough. He says, "Naw.

Who wants to shoot at stumps? I'm going hunting with this, soon as the season opens. Man, I'm going to shoot at some *live* targets!"

Big talk, which you should listen to with some sympathy even if you don't believe a word of it. Big talk is always a cover up for a small feeling of some kind, and in Joe's case it's a plain feeling of exhaustion.

You shot your 20-pound bow, Joe shot his 45. You both shot 40 arrows. You pulled a total weight of 800 pounds. But Joe? He pulled 1800 pounds! Add that shot he took to demonstrate his bow, and the practice draws he made. How many in all? Five? Well, poor old Joe actually pulled over a ton! No wonder he's tired, his fingers are cramped and his arm is sore. No wonder he couldn't hit a thing after the first couple of targets.

NAW! WHO WANTS TO SHOOT AT STUMPS?

Say goodbye to Joe, as a member of the gang. His pride will not allow him to admit the mistake of being overbowed, but to use the bow is hard work. So archery is no longer fun, for Joe.

The best weight of bow to have is the weight you can handle most easily. You should not have to think about the amount of strength you're using in drawing the bow. You should be able to concentrate on technique, and on aim.

So let sense be your guide and get a light bow that can become part of you as you learn to be an expert field archer. Start with 20 pounds. Even this weight can drive a field point through light gauge steel at 10 yards, so be careful.

Length of the bow is less important than proper weight. Take the length of your arm and double it as a rough measure. The bow should not be shorter than that, nor should it be taller than you are. Get a length that feels comfortable.

You will also be faced with a choice of bow style. There are two general styles, straight and reflex, or recurve. The amount of recurve varies considerably.

REFLEX or RECURVED

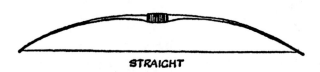

STRAIGHT

The recurved bow is more sensitive than the straight bow, which means that it is harder to shoot accurately. It does cast an arrow faster, pound for pound, than the straight bow, but this is no advantage if the archer can't hit the target. On the other hand, recurve bows are so common that it is sometimes difficult to get the standard straight bow, especially in the lower price ranges.

When you get to be an expert, the recurved bow may help you to break records—or it may keep you from it. But for beginners, the straight bow is definitely recommended.

To take care of your bow, keep it waxed, never leave it on the ground to be stepped on, do not leave it braced (strung), and be sure your string is in good shape at all times.

The illustrations show how to brace your bow.

Be careful not to dig the end into the dirt. If done properly, the end of the bow doesn't touch the ground at all.

We haven't mentioned arrows, but they have much to do with accuracy, and with safety.

The first thing about arrows is length. If an arrow is too short it can be overdrawn—pulled back beyond the bow handle. Then, if released, it will slam into the back of the bow, splintering and perhaps causing serious wounds. You wouldn't overdraw purposely, of course, but it can be done accidently, too. So the best thing is to get arrows long enough.

There are two ways of determining the best arrow length for you. One is to make a full draw with an arrow that is too long, and have a friend mark where it extends beyond the bow. Measure, and you have the proper length. Or, take a long arrow, a yardstick or anything suitable, place it against the upper part of your chest and stretch both hands out as far as you can. Where your fingertips meet is the mark for proper arrow length. Do not include the head in measuring.

An arrow that is too long will confuse your aim somewhat, but it is better to have arrows that are too long than arrows that are too short.

Arrows come in even sizes, the most common

being 26- and 28-inch arrows. They can also be bought in 24-, 22-, 20-, 18- and 30-inch lengths, but are much harder to find.

There are three types of points on arrows: target, field and hunting. Within these three types are variations, with the hunting heads varying the most.

Target points are most common. They are good only for soft targets, of straw or paper.

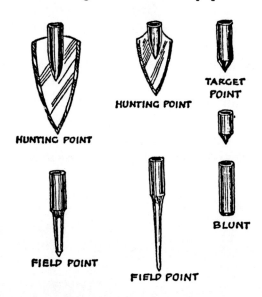

HUNTING POINT

HUNTING POINT

TARGET POINT

BLUNT

FIELD POINT

FIELD POINT

Hunting points are next most common. Do not buy them. Do not allow them in the house, unless you are old enough to hunt legally, with a qualified adult. In that case, you will know how to take care of your broadheads. Do not shoot with anyone who uses hunting points for field archery, unless it is a "broadhead round" on an established course under proper club auspices.

Why all the "don'ts"? Because a hunting broad-head of the proper design, properly shot, will not stop if it should hit someone. It is capable of going right through several inches of living *bone*. A good, well-cared-for broadhead can be used to shave with. It has a needle point. It is in all respects the equivalent of a razor blade combined with a needle-pointed stiletto. It is not a toy; it is a weapon designed to kill and not usable for anything else. A hunting point that does not meet these specifications isn't good enough to be used for hunting and therefore has no purpose at all.

Field points, the most difficult to find, are the ones you want. They can be used for soft targets, but they will also stick into stumps, boards and other hard targets.

Field arrows are usually a little heavier than target arrows. They're designed to take more of a beating.

When you shoot an arrow remember Newton's Laws. It's the arrow's inertia that breaks its head off when you shoot at the wrong target. The head stops because it can't penetrate any further. The shaft wants to keep going because it has considerable inertia. So the shaft, being of wood that's softer than the metal head, compresses into the head and weakens the whole area. A couple more shots and the head will break off.

Shoot only at suitable targets. It will help to save arrows.

Incidentally, if a properly designed and cared for hunting point is shot into a log or tree you can forget it. It will penetrate so deeply it must be cut out with a knife, which ruins both arrow and whatever it stuck into. If this should happen because you ignore the advice to stay away from hunting points, or because some foolish friend used them, break off the shaft and drive the head in.

What are you doing shooting at trees anyway? You should know better! The hole left by an arrow point is an entryway for bugs and disease. A small hole can kill a tree. No good woodsman mistreats a tree any more than he mistreats animals.

Arrows are not inexpensive. They can be bought for as little as 25 cents each, with target heads and unpainted shafts, but it's a miracle if you find a straight one. As a matter of statistics, consider yourself lucky if you can find straight arrows at all. Sight along the arrow and twirl it to see if it's straight. A crooked shaft won't travel a straight path, nor will a curved one.

Arrows can be straightened by heating over a hot plate and gently forcing them back into shape while warm, but this is hard work. Start with straight ones if you can.

Many archery supply stores carry field points for about ten cents each. If you can't get field arrows, or can't afford them, get field points and replace the target heads as they break off.

Arrows get lost, they break, and they lose heads and feathers. Lost heads and feathers can be replaced. Save broken arrows for replacement parts. Break splintered arrows. They're unsafe. Never try to tape one or glue it together again. The risk isn't worth it.

There are other pieces of equipment an archer needs, so let's cover them briefly.

A quiver is essential in field archery. A back-type quiver is more Robin-Hoodlike, but a belt quiver is preferred by some archers. Quivers can be bought or made. A very serviceable one can be made from a heavy cardboard mailing tube. Close one end with a wooden disk, and paint or cover with plastic. The references at the end of the chapter have some plans for making quivers. A ground quiver is handy when practicing on a single target. Make one out of a mailing tube or use an old umbrella stand.

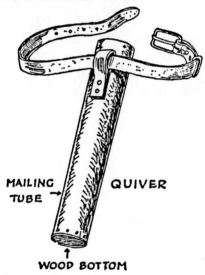

MAILING TUBE →   QUIVER

↑
WOOD BOTTOM

An arm guard is pretty important. A bowstring can actually strip a layer of skin off your forearm. More often it leaves a pink welt that is really a burn. Arm guards prevent this, but they also help

to improve accuracy by giving a smooth surface
from which the bowstring can glance without
catching. Arm guards can be bought or made.

ARM GUARD

Finger protectors, finger cots, tabs are names for
important little devices that help your shooting a
great deal. According to some books, tabs can be
made satisfactorily, but at their best they do not
compare with the commercially-made finger cots.
The purpose is not primarily to protect your fingers. Finger protectors, whether tabs or cots, are
most important in allowing the smooth release
which is essential for accuracy.

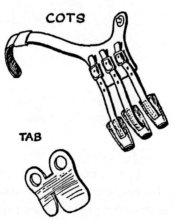

COTS

TAB

Bow strings come with bows, naturally enough. But there comes a time when the string wears out and must be replaced. You can make your own. Nearly every book on archery tells how. Or, you can buy a replacement. If you do, be sure it is made for the weight of your bow. Bowstrings should be whipped, and whipping should be heavy enough to hold the arrow without any help from your fingers. If your bowstring isn't whipped, whip it! Follow the same procedure given in Chapter II.

Beeswax is important to your string. You can buy a cake at most any hardware store. It will last indefinitely. Run it over your bowstring often. The string should be heavily waxed.

There are other items of equipment that can be brought or made, including Robin Hood-type archer's caps, shooting gloves of finest deerskin; belt pouches for carrying extra bowstrings, wax, and your finger protectors and arm guard when not in use; bow quivers that hold a few arrows for fast action, and so on. Some are fun to have, but none are really needed.

You will need targets. You will not need to buy them. Old newspapers are the archer's best friend if targets have to be improvised. If you live on a farm where hay is baled, you won't have to improvise because a bale of hay is the perfect target.

Nowdays vegetables and fruits come in bags made of string or plastic. These can be packed hard with crumpled newspaper and hung up as targets. Old flour or sugar sacks can be used in the same way, if that's how supplies are bought at your house. Burlap bags make fine targets when stuffed with crumpled newspapers.

Cardboard cartons can also be stuffed, sealed and used. They come apart when rained on, so be guided accordingly. Several layers of corrugated cardboard stacked together make a good target, too.

You don't need rings for field archery. The familiar kind of target with its concentric rings is for the target archer. The field archer shoots at any design. Animal cutouts are often used on field archery courses. You can make your own of oilcloth or plastic if you want to be fancy. Or, a small scrap of red cloth tacked to bag or target will serve as the animal's heart.

Now you're equipped and ready for the games of field archery. There are many variations, but a few are basic.

Rovers already has been described. The first
target is selected, and the archer hitting it best, or
coming closest, selects the next target. Of course
the shooting is from target to target—shoot, go
and collect arrows, shoot to next target, and so on.
The game can go on indefinitely, or until all arrows are lost or broken. Soft sand, rotted stumps
or logs, grass clumps, old corn shocks or hay bales
are the targets for the game of rovers.

Archery golf is great fun. It is played on a
golf course, or a course specially created for the
purpose. The idea is to "hole out" with the least
number of "strokes." The archery equivalent of
a hole-in-one would be a single shot from the tee
to the small archery target near the cup.

For archery golf, the cup into which the golfer
must put his ball is supplemented by a disk or
a soft ball on a low stake. The archer puts his final
shot into it. If his arrow lands within its own

length from the ball or disk the rest is conceded, as in the case of a near miss in golf.

Archery golf is played by experts with special bows and arrows, but it can be played equally well with an ordinary bow and a single arrow. If you go around nine holes in 30 shots or less, you're doing very well.

Clouts is a very old game. A huge target with rings like those of a standard target is drawn on the ground. The outer ring is 48 feet in diameter. The archer shoots 36 arrows from a distance of 180 yards. In the related game of Battle Clouts the target is smaller, 12 yards across, and the distance is increased to 200 yards.

(If the number 36 sounds odd, it's because we haven't explained up to this point that six arrows are one "end," and six "ends" is a common number.)

But of all games played with bow and arrow, the field round is the most fun. It is shot on a field archery course. Such courses are common across the country now, operated by field archery clubs.

Courses are designed to make the various shots as interesting as possible, and as natural as the terrain allows. The archer shoots around the course much as he plays around a golf course, but with several differences. He shoots four arrows at each target. He shoots from a whole variety of distances, across gullies, streams, up hillsides and through woods. His targets range in size from six inches in diameter to 24 inches in diameter.

In a standard round the archer shoots 96 arrows at either 28 targets or at 14 targets twice. As nine holes make a course in golf, 14 targets make a round in field archery. Some courses have two rounds of 14 targets each for a total of 28 targets. Others have only 14 targets which must be used twice.

If there is a field archery course near you, by all means see about joining the club and using it. If not, and you have enough room, make your own. It need not be a standard course. It can be as few as four targets or as many as room allows. You can make a course by placing vegetable bags stuffed with newspaper, or you can make a regulation course with bales of hay. Distances can vary from 10 yards to 80 yards.

There is a secret to being a successful field archer, and it's a pretty simple one that can be summed up in a few words: *A smooth release from a solid anchor point.*

Let's break this down and see what it means.

First of all, the way you hold the bowstring is important. The traditional kid's method of holding with thumb and forefinger won't do; it's unsafe and uncertain. You *must* use three fingers, in the so-called Mediterranean release. The string is held on the pads of the fingers, not on the joints. To release, it is only necessary to open the fingers.

Second, the bowstring should be whipped, and the nock of the arrow should fit on the whipping tightly enough so that it will not fall off if allowed to swing loose. This allows you to draw the string, without squeezing the arrow in your fingers. The arrow will follow the string. Lack of finger pressure on the arrow means a smoother shot.

Third, your grip on the bow should be loose. When spreading the bow you needn't put your fingers around the handle at all. The pressure should be on the fork of your hand, between

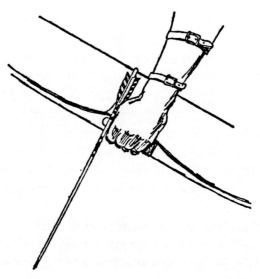

thumb and forefinger. You'll find that the bow
handle lays smoothly into this fork. A very loose
grip with your fingers will keep the bow from falling. By the way, use both hands to spread the bow.
Don't put one arm out and make the other one do
all the work of drawing the string. Make both
arms work, one pushing and the other pulling until the bow is spread.

Fourth, your anchor point should be a sensible,
comfortable one. Your anchor point is that point
on your face to which the nock of the arrow is
drawn *every time*. Repeat, *every time*. It doesn't
matter if the shot is short or long. The anchor
point remains unchanged. This is to make sure
that the bow shoots the same way every time. You
can't hope for consistent accuracy unless you
know how the bow shoots from your anchor point.

Field archers use a high anchor point, target
archers use a low one. The higher the anchor
point, the closer the archer is to sighting down the
arrow. But there is a limit to how high one can

get, and the limit is about the level of the nosetip.

A favorite anchor point is on the cheek, with the middle finger pressing on one particular spot. The big jaw muscle at the place where upper and lower jaws meet is convenient. Just ahead of this muscle is a handy pocket into which the middle finger can press. The thumb, which is not used, can help with the anchor point by curling behind the jawbone or ear and finding a spot for permanent reference.

ANCHOR POINT

Fifth, whether your stance is bent over, straight, kneeling or sitting, it should be solid.

Sixth, the release must be made simply by opening the fingers and letting the arrow go. The bow hand and arm do not move. The anchor hand stays anchored. It's good to practice the release paying attention only to the anchor hand. Keep it in place until the arrow has hit the target.

And that's about all there is to it.

Easy? No, not really. No sport is easy if you want to do it right, because it means practicing the fundamentals over and over again.

You draw to the anchor point and look at the spot on the target you intend to hit. You release smoothly. If your form is good, chances are you came close to hitting what you intended to hit. If your form isn't good, you may have come close anyway. But without good form on the hold and release, you cannot get consistent results.

As you practice, your instinct develops. You do instant calculating in your own brain without even knowing you're doing it. You figure distance, amount of elevation you need on your arrow, wind velocity and target motion, if any, all in the instant of drawing the bow. Your eye has all the data necessary for figuring the angle. You look at the target, but you also see the tip of your arrow by what is called peripheral vision. Your mind calculates the angle between the line of the arrow and the target, but you're not even aware of it.

WHAT THE FIELD
ARCHER SEES

Don't worry about distance. Worry only about form, and concentrating on the target. Nature will do the rest, if you practice enough and experiment enough.

You'll never bring home silver cups for target shooting, but someday you may bring home a bearskin rug with a hole in it made by your keen broadhead.

Even if you never hunt, it's a lot of fun. There are few things so satisfying as watching the perfect flight of an arrow and hearing the solid thunk of a dead-center hit.

If you decide to go in for it, your librarian has books on archery. You may, however, want to get some of your own.

The Boy Scout handbook on Archery in the Merit Badge Series is helpful. It has hints on making equipment. However, the shooting method it describes and illustrates is for the target archer. Note that the Scouts on the pamphlet cover use different styles, and that one is not holding to an anchor point properly.

The Official Handbook of the National Field Archery Association is a gold mine of information. It costs a dollar and may be obtained by writing to the National Field Archery Association of the United States, Inc., PO Box 388, Redlands, California.

An exciting book by one of the greatest archers of modern times is Howard Hill's *Hunting The Hard Way*. It has been republished in a paperback edition under the title of *Howard Hill's Archery Adventures* by Trend Books.

A number of archery equipment companies publish booklets that they will be glad to send you for the asking. See the advertisements in sports magazines.

As in all sports, safety comes first, followed by fun. Field archery is more fun than most sports. It is, as the NFAA insignia says, *"The Sport of Men Since Time Began."*

Chapter VIII

Scotty's Tips On Tricks and Games

Scotty spent his time making an improvised game of Yoot, an ancient Korean game that can be played almost anywhere, under nearly any circumstances. At its simplest, the Yoot board can be scratched in the dirt with a stick, and the Yoot throwing sticks . . . can be cut from a twig.

from THE BLUE GHOST MYSTERY
Chapter VIII, *The Splitting Atoms.*

IT'S AS natural for Don Scott, called Scotty, to learn about games in a foreign country as it is for Rick Brant to learn about the country's science. Both boys have an abundance of curiosity, an interest in science, and a love of action. But there is a difference between them that may be expressed this way: Rick is more interested in *ideas*. Scotty is more concerned with *things*, and how they work.

In this chapter various interesting things Scotty has found are described for those with the same kind of interest. Some are to make, some are to do, and some are just to know about for future use.

Of course the best way to remember something is to learn it by doing. The things that appeal to you should be tried. Play Yoot with a pal, practice coordination with the electrical games, try the riddles on your parents and friends, and so on.

THE GAME OF YOOT

This is said to be a Korean game. It is certainly Oriental and very old. In pattern, it is related to the original "board" game, parchesi, which started in ancient Persia. Yoot may have developed independently in the Far East. Scotty learned it from Sing, the Spindrift party guide in THE CAVES OF FEAR.

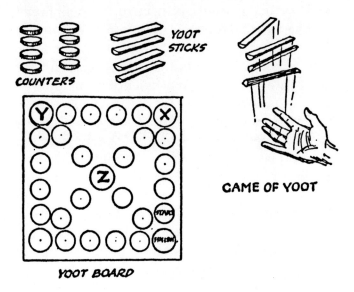

YOOT STICKS

COUNTERS

GAME OF YOOT

YOOT BOARD

The equipment for Yoot consists of a board, four counters for each player, and four Yoot sticks.

The Yoot sticks are made from straight twigs, split down the middle. A Yoot stick is three to four inches long, and has one flat side and one half-rounded side. Sticks can be made by sawing dowels, by splitting round pencils, or by splitting the shaft of a broken arrow.

Counters ("men" as they are called in board games) can be checkers, initialed pieces of paper, coins like four dimes for one player and four pennies for another, or easily identified pebbles.

The board can be painted on wood, sketched on a sheet of paper, or scratched in the bare earth.

On the trail with no equipment, for example, Yoot sticks can be cut from twigs with a jackknife, pebbles or bits of bark or twig used for counters, and the board scratched next to the campfire.

The board layout is shown in the drawing. Circles mark the positions. Rough X's would do just as well. Start, finish, two corners, and the center are labeled for convenience in the illustration. No labels are needed in actual play.

To start a counter on the board, it is necessary to get a Yoot. This is a throw of the sticks by one of the players in which all four flat sides land upwards. The sticks are held loosely in the hand and tossed into the air, being allowed to land freely.

A Yoot always calls for another throw by the same player, so he gets the four moves of the Yoot, plus the number of "flats" on the next throw. If all round sides come up, that's too bad. He has only his four original moves to make. The counter moves the number of positions shown by the flat sides.

A new counter can be started with any throw of a Yoot. Counters can move together. If a throw puts two counters in the same position, they can

move together from then on, like a king in checkers.

A player with more than one counter on the
board can move any of his counters, or split his
move between counters except when going to the
finish.

One player can pass another without penalty.
But if a player's counter lands on the position already occupied by another player, the counter
that was overtaken has to start over, with a
Yoot needed to restart.

As a counter nears the finish, the player must
throw the exact number of flats that will take him
past the finish and off the board. If a player lands
on finish, he must throw a one to get off.

The first player to get all counters off the board
is the winner.

Of course players alternate throws, except when
one gets a Yoot. Two or three can play. The board
becomes too crowded with four.

Now, refer to the board layout. If a counter
lands exactly on X, Y, or Z, the player's next
turn can take it down the shortest path to the
finish. If the number of flats thrown takes the
counter past these points, the long way around
must be followed. A counter that passes X still
has a chance to turn at Y if the right throws are
made. A counter that lands on X can turn down
the diagonal, turning again at Z if the correct
throws are made. If the throws are not made, the
counter continues down the diagonal to the corner
and takes the long route.

The board is easy to remember—six circles

along the edges, seven circles along the diagonals counting the corners.

And that's Yoot.

FINGER MULTIPLICATION

In the adventure of THE LOST CITY there was a brief period when Sahmeed, the Mongol guide, was friendly with the Spindrift group. During that time Scotty learned from Sahmeed an ancient method of using the fingers to multiply numbers from six through ten. Sahmeed had learned the method from a Kirghiz, who had learned it from a Kurd, who had learned it from a merchant in Samarkand. The system is still in use in some parts of Asia.

To use the system you must be able to add by ten and to multiply numbers from 1 to 5.

Start by assigning numbers to your fingers, counting your thumb as a finger. The little finger is 6, the ring finger 7, the middle finger 8, the forefinger 9, and the thumb 10. Check the drawing.

Suppose you want to multiply 8 by 7. Put the tip of the 7 finger of one hand (either one) against the tip of the 8 finger of the other hand.

Hold your hands in front of you and count with your eyes.

The fingers that are touching, and all fingers below them count for 10 each. Add them up. You'll get 50.

Remember that the thumb counts as a finger. Count the fingers on each hand above the ones that are touching, and multiply the fingers on one hand by the fingers on the other. In this example, one hand will have 3 fingers above the touching ones and the other hand will have 2. $2 \times 3 = 6$. Add this to the number you got by counting in tens. $50 + 6 = 56$. The correct answer is 56.

This kind of multiplying with your own digits takes longer to explain than to do. Try another example. Multiply 9 by 8.

Forefinger on one hand touches middle finger on the other. These two plus all below add up to 7 tens, or 70. Above the touching fingers are 2 on one hand and only 1 on the other. $2 \times 1 = 2$. Add and get the correct answer: 72.

Prove the system by multiplying 6 by 6. Touch little fingers. The remaining fingers on each hand number 4. $4 \times 4 = 16$. Each little finger is worth 10: 20 plus 16 gives the correct answer: 36.

If you haven't succeeded in memorizing your multiplication tables, this little trick can be useful. Think how useful it would be to a nine-fingered Martian! Anyway, in these days when digital computers make news, you can tell your friends you carry a digital computer around with you—and use your own digits to prove it.

THE ELECTRIC RAPIER

Scotty once rigged up a device for practice in coordination, and to check hand and eye. He became so interested in using it that he and Rick looked into the art of fencing and used the device to practice lunges and thrusts.

The device was an electrified rapier, which is a very slim dueling sword, with a target.

The basis for the rapier and target was a simple electrical circuit. In the drawing, notice that the only parts to the circuit are a battery, a signal, and a key that acts as a switch. When the switch is closed the signal operates. When the switch is opened, it stops.

A buzzer makes the best signal because it sounds so loudly and suddenly that the operator jumps. But a visual signal—a simple flashlight bulb—also can be used.

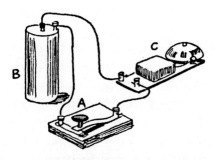

Scotty used a coat hanger, a sheet of soft aluminum of the kind sold at most hardware stores, a buzzer from one of Rick's old electrical toy kits, and a flashlight battery.

The aluminum sheet was marked with holes of

various sizes and shapes, including circles and triangles, a heart and—at Barby Brant's suggestion —a Zorro Z. The designs were cut out of the aluminum by starting a cut with a cold chisel and finishing it with a pair of tinsmith's snips. At the top edge of the aluminum sheet Scotty put a pair of holes, so the sheet could be suspended by a pair of wires.

He straightened out the coat hanger, after cutting off the hook and the twisted wire. The now straight wire was sandpapered until all finish was removed and bright metal showed through.

Scotty cut a four-inch length from an old broomstick and drilled a hole through it length-wise. The hole was just big enough to take the wire. He pushed the wire through so the broomstick formed a handle. Just enough wire projected beyond it for soldering on several feet of thin, flexible insulated wire.

The other end of the wire from his coat hanger rapier was connected to one terminal of the battery. From the other battery terminal a length of wire was run to a terminal on the buzzer. To the other buzzer terminal a six-foot length of wire ran to the aluminum sheet where it was soldered into place.

If you study the drawing, you can see that the electrical hookup is identical to the simple circuit of buzzer, battery and switch. The rapier and the aluminum target take the place of the switch. When the rapier touches the target the circuit is closed, current flows and the buzzer sounds.

Scotty hung the aluminum sheet by two wires,

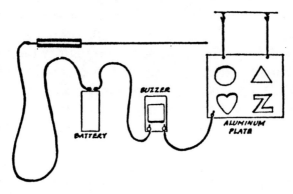

with battery and buzzer lying on the floor under
it. Then he took a fencer's stance in front of the
target and tried to put the tip of his rapier into
the various designs without touching the metal.
Silence indicated success. A loud buzz sounded
failure.

Many variations are possible in this simple
game. Here are some of them:

Sheet aluminum is expensive. Look for a substitute. It must be a good conductor of electricity.
If you use frozen dinners in your house, the trays
can be used to make targets.

Buzzers that operate from flashlight battery current come in electrical construction sets and in some toys like electric jackstraws. If you can't locate one, doorbell buzzers can be used. However, these take a higher voltage. Ten volts is common. Such buzzers cost around a dollar. They are operated by transformers that plug into 110 volt house current. Transformers cost over two dollars.

It isn't necessary to use a buzzer. A light can signal a miss, too. Most hardware stores have small sockets for flashlight bulbs. These can be mounted with small machine screws right on the target itself. They cost about 15 cents.

Covering a cardboard target with aluminum foil can be made to work. Be sure the foil covers the inside edges of the target cutouts, because that's where the rapier strikes most. Tape on the back of such a cardboard target will hold the foil in place.

If you can't solder, wrap the rapier connecting wire around the coat hanger wire as tightly as you can, and either tape it in place or secure it with a metallic glue or cement. The target wire can be secured to sheet metal with a sheet metal screw. Make a hole slightly smaller than the screw. If you use a cardboard target with aluminum foil, secure the wire with a small machine screw (screw and nut) and put a clean washer under the screw head to make good contact with the foil.

Finally, you can reverse the whole thing and arrange the device so that the signal flashes or sounds when the rapier touches the desired target. The simplest way of doing this is to use a small disk of metal with wire connected. Let the disk hang from the wire. If you use this method it is also possible to make a rapier of wood. Run the connecting wire along the wood to the rapier tip. Tape the wire in place every few inches. To the rapier tip secure a disk of metal with a screw. Wrap the connecting wire around the screw under the disk and tighten into place.

There is only one problem in making such a device, apart from the ever-present possible poor connections. That is, the voltage drop through the metal sheet, the long wires and the rapier may be so great that not enough current reaches the signal to operate it. Scotty's worked fine, because he used a fairly small target, about 12 by 18 inches, and his connections were electrically sound. If yours doesn't, another battery in the circuit, in series, will do the trick.

Like most of us, you have probably imagined yourself with sword, cutlass, rapier, saber or machete in hand cutting away at a hostile savage or other enemy. The target won't strike back, but it will certainly let you know how real your fancies were as you cut down that pirate with one sure thrust!

THREADING THE ROD

The electrical circuit used in the rapier and target arrangement can be adapted to the kind of game that's fun at parties or other gatherings. It's a test of coordination and steadiness.

Scotty used a piece of wood for a base. It was about a foot long and four inches wide. He drilled a hole, just big enough to take a coat hanger wire, through a small block of wood and mounted it on the board by nailing through from the bottom. The hole for the wire was about an inch above the board.

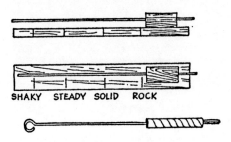

SHAKY   STEADY   SOLID   ROCK

A coat hanger was cut into two one-foot lengths. These were sanded until shiny and clean. One was pushed through the hole in the block, leaving just enough projecting past the block to make a connection. The long part was bent until it was parallel to the board.

The other wire was bent at one end to form a round eye. Scotty did this by using pliers and a hammer to force the wire around a thin metal rod. He could have used a spike for the same purpose. The eye should be no less than twice the diameter of the coat hanger wire, and not more than three times the diameter.

To the other end of this wire a flexible connecting wire was soldered, then a handle was formed by wrapping the coat hanger wire with tape.

The illustration shows the completed layout. You can see that the wire with the eye and the one projecting from the block now form the switch in the electrical circuit. A length of paper with scoring boxes is mounted on the board under the wire.

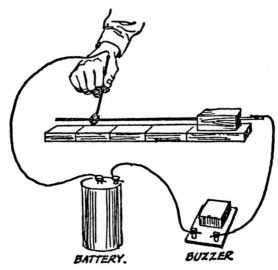

BATTERY.   BUZZER

The object, of course, is to pass the eye up the projecting wire without causing the signal to operate. Those who get the rating of "Rock" (for rock steady) can improve their standing by putting the eye up the wire and removing it again without touching. This deserves a rating of "Double Rock" at the very least.

THOUGHT TWISTERS

Scotty enjoys riddles, but they must be the kind that requires a genuine solution rather than the kind that is a joke. There are many of the type, and they all have one thing in common: the riddle must contain all the information that is necessary to solve it. Scotty's favorites are these:

Amoeba in a bowl. It's a well known fact of nature that the lowly amoeba multiplies by what is called binary fission. One amoeba splits to form two. After a period of growth each of those split to form two more, for a total of four. Eventually the four split, although not all at the same time, and form eight, and so on.

Now, suppose all amoebae split at the same time, and they do this once every second. Of course they don't, but this is a riddle, not a treatise on zoology, so let's suppose.

We start with one amoeba in a bowl. In the first second it splits and forms two. In the second second the two split and form four. In the third second the four split and form eight. This keeps on until the bowl is full of amoebae.

The bowl is full in 50 seconds.

When is it half full?

Most people work too hard to solve this one if they fail to see the solution right away. They try to figure it out mathematically, and 25 seconds is the answer most often given—which is wrong.

Remember, *all* amoebae in the problem split once each second, so the answer is: the bowl is half full in 49 seconds. In the next second each amoeba splits, and presto! Full bowl.

The explorer and the bear. An explorer sets up camp. He decides to go hunting. He walks 15 miles due south, but sees no game. He turns and walks 15 miles due west—and sees a bear. He shoots the bear. With the bear slung on his back (He's as strong as Zircon, the giant Spindrift scientist) he walks 15 miles due north and arrives at his camp again.

What color is the bear?

The bear is white. It has to be a polar bear, because the only place where you could follow the path the explorer took is at the North Pole.

The elevator buttons. A man lives on the ninth floor of an apartment building. The building has a self-operated elevator which the residents operate by pushing the proper button for the floor they want.

Each morning the man gets on the elevator and pushes the first-floor button. Each evening, as he returns from work he pushes the seventh-floor button, gets off at the seventh floor and walks up two flights to his apartment on the ninth. Every once in a while he rides all the way to the ninth floor.

Can you explain his actions?

Review the data. He pushes the buttons for the seventh and first floors. Sometimes he rides to the ninth floor—no mention of button pushing.

Usually the explanation offered is that he needs exercise, he visits a friend on the seventh floor, or that he's eccentric. All wrong. The explanation is much simpler.

The man is a midget. In the morning he can reach the first-floor button. At night, reaching his highest, he can only reach the seventh-floor button. Sometimes a ninth-floor neighbor gets on at the same time and pushes the button, and the midget is able to ride all the way.

The hunter and the squirrel. The hunter walks through the woods and sees a squirrel on a tree, too far away for a shot. The hunter walks closer. The squirrel goes around the tree to the other side, putting the trunk between him and the hunter. The hunter can no longer see the squirrel.

The hunter goes around the tree. The squirrel scampers around the trunk, always keeping out of sight of the hunter.

The hunter goes around the tree. The squirrel is on the tree.

Does the hunter go around the squirrel?

There is no catch in this one. It is a matter of straightforward logic. Visualize it this way: Two bugs are on a wagon wheel rim, at the ends of spokes that are directly opposite each other. They can't see each other because the axle is in the way. Do the bugs go around each other as the wheel revolves? No, and for the same reason, the hunter does not go around the squirrel even though he goes around the tree. If this still doesn't seem reasonable, look at it this way. The squirrel could keep out of the hunter's sight by moving around the tree on the ground, not touching the tree at all.

Dick Turpin and the judge. This is not really a riddle because it poses a problem with no solution, but it's fun to try it on people just to see whether they decide there is none.

Long ago, the town of London was overrun with highwaymen, footpads, cutpurses and other thieves. The City Council took action and started a kind of dragnet that most of the thieves escaped by leaving London—which was what the Council wanted.

To prevent the thieves from returning, the Council closed all entrances to the town except for London Bridge. On the bridge they stationed a squad of watchmen, a judge, and a hangman complete with gallows.

The watchmen stopped everyone crossing the bridge. The judge asked two questions: "Where are you going? What are you going to do there?" If the judge decided the answers were truthful, the voyager was allowed to pass. If the judge decided the answers were lies, the watchmen grabbed the victim and the hangman went into action.

The system worked just fine, until one day a famous highwayman, Dick Turpin, came to the bridge. The watchmen grabbed him, for Turpin was well known. The judge, rubbing his hands at this opportunity to get rid of the daring and notorious Turpin, asked the questions. The hangman got his rope ready.

"Where are you going? What are you going to do there?"

And Turpin answered, "I'm going to yonder gallows, and I'm going to be hanged."

Now, if Turpin went to the gallows and was hanged, he would be telling the truth—and truthful men were allowed to pass. If he was allowed to pass, he would be lying—and liars were hanged.

There was nothing in the Council's rules about letting the traveler go back to where he had come from.

History does not record the decision. What would you have done?

MAGIC WRITING

Scotty became interested in magic writing in Hongkong when he saw a Chinese magician perform an interesting trick.

The magician showed a blank piece of paper to his outdoor audience and announced that he would use the sun itself to show them some of the great wisdom of Lao-Tse. He then produced an ordinary magnifying glass of the reading glass type and focused the sun's rays on the paper. As the focus moved across the paper Chinese characters appeared.

Scotty couldn't read Chinese, but from the crowd's reaction he guessed the Chinese magician had succeeded.

The trick, as Scotty learned, was very simple. Dip a clean steel pen into lemon juice and write. Let the paper dry and the writing is invisible. Heat the paper as the Chinese did with the magnifying glass, and the writing appears.

Other liquids that can be used in the same way are onion juice, milk, vinegar, and grapefruit juice. All are "sympathetic inks," which means they can be developed by heating.

The simplest way of developing sympathetic inks is to iron the paper as you would a piece of cloth, with a heated flatiron.

Ordinary household starch and iodine can be used to produce a very effective kind of secret ink. Dissolve starch in warm water and let it cool. Write with the starch solution, always using a clean pen. Dilute iodine to make a developer. Iodine comes in a water (aqueous) solution, an alcohol (tincture) solution, and in a special kind of chemical with a long name abbreviated to PVP. Dilution has to be with the proper solvent. If you have trouble, don't dilute, but use a brush to make a thin film of iodine on the paper. The writing will appear as a bluish purple.

Starch and iodine always act this way together. Touch a bit of iodine to a cracker and see what happens. The color produced is proof that the cracker contains starch. Iodine is a very old test for the presence of starch.

Salt can be used for secret writing, too. A solution of salt and water forms the ink. Dissolve ordinary table salt in warm water until no more will go into solution. When the writing is dry it can be developed by shading the paper with a soft lead pencil. Where the salt is left by the evaporating water, the paper is rougher, and so more lead rubs off, leaving a dark line.

A number of chemicals can be used in secret writing, too. Many of them are found in inexpensive chemistry sets. One chemical forms the ink, the other the developer. The same chemical reactions are used in turning "water" to ink, turning "water" to "wine" and turning colored liquid into clear liquid again. The chemistry sets have the necessary instructions.

There is little practical use for secret writing except as "magic," but it's fun to know and to try. Besides, if you should ever be captured it would be useful to know how to write a secret cry for help with some of the foods served in your prison.

The only problem in such a situation is that the person receiving an apparently innocent letter with secret writing between the lines might not have any idea the letter was more than it seemed, or not know how to develop the message.

On second thought, better not get captured. Too risky.

TRANSFER SOLUTION

When Barby Brant tried to find a new way to use newspaper photos in a scrapbook without the bulkiness caused by pasting actual clippings, Scotty found the answer. He mixed one part turpentine with four parts of water. Since the two liquids will not mix without help, he added a pea-sized bit of soap and shook the solution until the soap dissolved. The soap created an emulsion—which is what soap is supposed to do.

Barby copied newspaper photos by moistening them with the mixture, placing a clean sheet of paper on the photo, and rubbing hard with the side of a small jar. Newspaper ink was dissolved by the emulsion (with the turpentine as the active agent) and transferred to the paper. She was pleased with the photos but upset by the printed matter, which came out backwards, naturally enough.

The mixture will work with newspaper and comic book cartoons, too.

Much of travel, glamorous though it may be, consists of waiting. Either the waiting is for train, ship, bus, plane, car or oxcart to arrive, or the waiting is for a destination to be reached.

Scotty has found several forms of amusement to help pass the time on trips. They help keep him busy, they provide games to play with a companion, and they provide openings for conversations with fellow travelers. Scotty has even used them to quiet noisy children, thus doing a service to the entire train car or busload of passengers. A few minutes at any stop will provide most of the materials needed.

THE GEE-HAW WHIMIDIDDLE

Scotty learned about this gadget from the Indians of North Carolina.

Dry pieces of twig are needed, preferably of a medium-hard wood. Soft wood will not do. The twigs should be about a quarter inch in diameter. Two six-inch lengths and one two-inch length will serve.

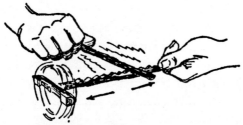

GEE-HAW-WHIMIDIDDLE

One twig forms the body. It is cut flat at one end. About an inch and a half from that end, notches are cut to form a continuous series of humps. The notches should be about an eighth of an inch deep and slightly wider at the top than at the bottom. Eight notches is about right. Leave enough twig below the notches to form a grip.

The second long twig forms a scraper. It is only necessary to remove the bark from one end. If the twig has a natural handle, so much the better.

The third piece of twig forms the spinner. Cut the ends flat, trimming the piece to about an inch and one-quarter in length. Cut it as shown in the illustration. Drill a hole in the middle of the flat side with the awl blade of your Scout knife. The hole should be large enough so it will be loose on the shaft you use.

The small twig is now a spinner. It is connected to the flat end of the body twig by any shaft at hand. A small screw is best. A small nail is next best. If a pin must be used, drill the hole with the pin, working it in the hole until the spinner can move freely. Beware of splitting the twig. Work carefully.

When you are finished, the spinner should spin freely when you tap one end with a finger.

To operate, hold the notched twig at a slight angle upwards. Rub the notches with the other twig. After you get the hang of it, the spinner will spin rapidly, like a miniature airplane propeller. You will be able to reverse the direction of spin, too.

Such things are as old as boys and jackknives in some parts of the country. The gee-haw-whimididdle name is from the North Carolina mountain country. Research has not disclosed what it means.

THE ESKIMO YO-YO

Scotty learned about this game during a trip to the Far North. He returned to the continental United States and enthusiastically described it to his friends, only to find that many of them knew about it and had even made such toys.

They are more common among the Eskimo kids, however, than in most parts of the United States. They are made of braided yarn strings and small leather bags or drums, weighted and elegantly decorated with fur, beads, and colored yarn. It seems likely that the Eskimos learned about them from white men, but where the idea originally came from is a mystery.

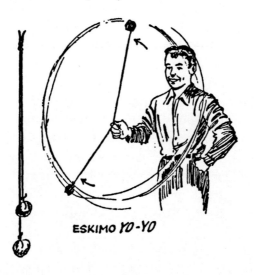

ESKIMO YO-YO

In the continental United States the Eskimo Yo-Yo's are generally made in the fall from two horse chestnuts and a piece of strong string four or five feet long. Holes are bored in the chestnuts with a nail, awl blade or twig and the string ends tied through. They can be made from any small weights, including fishing sinkers, washers, pieces of wood, or a few pebbles in small pieces of cloth.

The weights are attached to the ends of the string. The string is held with weights dangling, so one weight is a couple of inches lower than the other. A knot is then tied in the string to form a finger grip.

The idea is to get the two weights counter-rotating (rotating in opposite directions). They are kept going as long as possible. But the trick is to get them started.

One way is to stretch the weights apart on the ground in front of you. Grip the finger knot and lift rapidly. Gravity will move the weights toward each other, and up and down hand motions will keep them going.

The second method is to take the knot in hand, hold one weight with the other hand, and start the hanging weight rotating. With proper timing, toss the held weight into motion in the opposite direction.

A gentle up and down hand motion keeps the weights rotating until they collide, and a new start must be made.

THE TOWERS OF HANOI

The Towers of Hanoi are three spindles. On one is a stack of counters, each one smaller than the one under it.

The object is to transfer the stack from one

tower to another without ever putting a larger counter on a smaller one.

According to legend, Buddhist monks in a secret lamasery are even now working on a project to transfer a stack of 64 golden disks from one tower to another. They have been working since the time of Buddha. When all counters are transferred, the world will end in a mighty thunderclap.

This probably will cause you considerable worry, but please be reassured. The project will take millions of years, even with the monks working in relays at top speed.

Scotty learned this game from Chahda, a one-time Bombay beggar boy and close friend of the Spindrift group. Chahda learned it from a Buddhist monk. He says the monk is one of those working on the project to finish off the world, but it's hard to know when Chahda is joking.

THE TOWERS OF HANOI

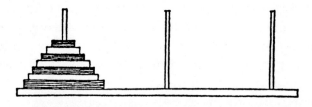

The Towers of Hanoi can be made at home from square pieces of wood that are graduated in size. A lath, piece of orange crate, or any thin wood will serve. Size doesn't matter. Seven counters will do, or you can make ten if you're very ambitious.

Start with a strip of wood. Saw off a 2-inch piece. Then saw off a 1¾-inch piece. Then a 1½-inch piece. Continue, with each piece a quarter inch smaller than the preceding one, until the final piece is ½-inch wide.

Stack the pieces in order, smallest on top. Color or otherwise mark every other one. This is to help you solve the puzzle.

(If you want a ten-counter group, start with a 3-inch piece and end up with a ¾-inch piece.)

Get a piece of board for a base. Drive three large nails completely through it. The two outer nails should be at least 4 inches from the center nail (or 6 inches for a ten-counter game).

File off the sharp nail tip.

Use a drill with a quarter-inch diameter and drill right down through the centers of your stacked counters. Place them on one of the outside towers. That's all there is to it.

Fancier versions can be made, of course, using dowels as towers and graduated disks as counters.

Towers of Hanoi can be purchased, too.

Scotty makes sets two ways while traveling. The counters are the same for both. They are made from rectangles of cardboard, cut out with a sharp jackknife. In the center of the rectangles slits large enough to fit over the towers are cut out. Cardboard seems always to be around when traveling, usually a leftover container from someone's lunch, or from the meal the airline stewardess provides.

The towers are made from cardboard by cutting three strips in a rectangle of cardboard and bending them upright. Or, towers can be made from a bent coat hanger. The twisted hook end can be broken off by working the wire back and forth until the metal fatigues and breaks.

To work the tower game, start with the counters stacked in order. The secret of success is never to put two counters of the same color together. This is the reason for identifying alternate ones by painting, shading with a pencil, or marking in some way.

Notice that the number of moves necessary to change a single counter grows greater as you move down the stack. That's why you need not worry too much about the world's ending in a thunderclap. Your great-great grandchildren a thousand generations from now may see the end, but you won't.

It would be interesting to know for certain whether or not the world really will end as the sixty-fourth counter drops into place, wouldn't it?

TICK TACK TOE BACKWARDS

Few boys pass the age of eight without learning tick tack toe, but in case you are one of them or your memory needs jogging, here's the diagram:

One player takes O and the other takes X. The play alternates, with each player making his mark in a cell of the diagram. Each player tries to get three marks in a row, across, down, or diagonally, while preventing the other player from doing the same thing. The player who makes it, wins.

Scotty learned the backwards version from Professor Julius Weiss, the Spindrift mathematician, who also gave him a tip on winning.

In reverse tick tack toe the object is backwards. The player who gets three in a row is the loser.

Curiously, the backwards game is more complex than the frontwards version.

This is what Julius Weiss told Scotty, after winning ten out of ten games: If the first player opens in any box but the center one, the second player can always win. Each time be sure to allow your opponent the greatest number of chances to put three in a row.

If you're the first player, put your mark in the center cell. From then on, match your opponent's move by putting your mark directly opposite his. The game will end in a draw.

Chapter IX

Rick's Scientific Experiments

As they entered Rick's room, Scotty stopped short, his glance taking in the weird assortment of gadgets.

"Come in," Rick said. "I'll explain the place to you."

"You'll have to. What is it, an electrical museum?"

"Brant Hall of Electronic Science," Rick replied.
from THE ROCKET'S SHADOW
Chapter IV, *Scotty Gets Himself a Job*.

RICK'S FIRST love is electronics and its parent, the science of physics. But, like most boys, his interests are wide. At various times he has delved into most of the sciences, usually working up an experiment or two, and reading one or two books as an introduction to the subject.

This chapter describes several experiments Rick has performed in electronics and other aspects of science. However, Rick didn't simply stop with the experiment. In every case he took the trouble to look up a few references, and in most cases one experiment led to another. What you do about these experiments is, of course, mostly a matter of how interested you become in the subject. Try them. If you find that you want to do other, similar experiments, there are many good books on whatever subject interests you.

EXPERIMENT IN TOPOLOGY

We lead off with an experiment on topology for two reasons. First of all, you can do it right now with equipment you have in the house. Second, it will show you that even the simplest of things has its strange elements, and that, in science, things are not always what they seem.

Topology has been called "the geometry of distortion." It is concerned with the relationships of surfaces and spaces. Topologists, however, have a somewhat different view of things than most of us. For instance, are you a doughnut?

You are probably convinced that you are not a doughnut, even though you may have eaten too many for breakfast. But, to a topologist, the human form and a doughnut have much in common. You can find the reasons for this, if you're interested.

Our experiment in topology, however, takes us into the strange realm of two dimensions. Until now, your experience with two dimensions has probably been limited to shadows. A shadow is truly two dimensional because it can have length and width, but it cannot have the third dimension that allows it to have a volume, or depth.

You will need: at least two long strips of paper about one and a half inches wide (the width isn't important so long as it's enough to work with) and from two to three feet long. Such strips can be cut from wrapping paper, a big paper bag, or —if there's nothing better around—the margin of a newspaper. You will also need scissors, celluloid tape, and a soft pencil or crayon.

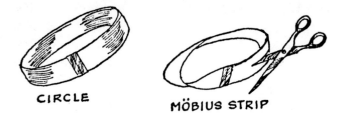

CIRCLE   MÖBIUS STRIP

Start by making a paper ring from one strip. Examine it, and think about it. You've seen such paper rings before, but have you ever considered their properties? The ring has an inside and an outside. In other words, it has two surfaces. If asked to paint one pink and the other blue, you could do it.

Suppose you placed the ring on a table and put a pencil flat on the table in the center of the strip. By pulling the paper under the pencil you could make a line along the center of the paper until the line met itself again. Try it. You will see that the line covers only one side of the paper. The other side is still blank. Now, thrust the scissors into the line and cut along the line until you've reached the point where the scissors started. What do you have? Two strips of paper. Cut a two-sided object in half and you get two halves.

Now, use the other piece of paper, keeping in mind the things you "learned" from the paper circle. But this time, as you bring the ends together to join them, give one end a half turn. Just turn it over. Then stick the ends together with tape.

You have made a Möbius strip, named for the scientist who discovered it. A Möbius strip has only one surface. You doubt it? You can prove it.

Repeat the pencil line drawing. Just put the strip on the table and make the line by pulling the paper under the pencil. Keep going until the line meets itself.

Examine the paper. Is there any section of it that is without a section of line? You see that there isn't. You drew a continuous line through the middle of every inch of paper without lifting the pencil or crossing an edge. You can only do that with a one-sided surface. You can feel the thickness of the paper? That's an illusion. You can pick any section of the Möbius strip and have the illusion of a two-sided object with a line on both sides. But you know the line is on the same side, because you drew it without lifting the pencil or crossing an edge.

If you wish, you may now try to paint one side of the strip red and the other blue.

Finally, take the scissors, insert into the center line, and cut. If you have never seen a Möbius strip before, you have a surprise in store. Cut along the center line until you reach the starting point again. Amazing? Yes, but only in a three-dimensional world. Anything can happen in two dimensions. Make another strip and watch closely. Stop cutting just before the end and examine the strip. You will be able to see what happens, and why.

Once the cut is completed you no longer have a Möbius strip. Try to figure out what changed it back into a two-sided object again. Make another cut down the middle of the strip and see what happens.

There is an old magician's trick based on the Möbius strip. It's called the Arabian Turban. The magician allows two people from the audience to rip his turban right down the middle, and of course they fail to do it. Now you know why— don't you?

Rick followed the Möbius strip by making a Klein bottle, which is a bottle that has neither an inside nor an outside. You can do this too, if you find topology interesting. Look it up. As a hint, Rick made his out of a bicycle inner tube.

The next step beyond the Klein bottle is a tesseract, which is a four-dimensional cube. No one has yet succeeded in building such a cube, mostly because fourth-dimensional glue hasn't yet been invented.

EXPERIMENT IN CRYOGENICS

Cryogenics is the name given to the production and use of low temperatures. When scientists speak of cryogenic temperatures they are talking of the temperature of liquid helium. Such low figures cannot be obtained outside of the laboratory without complex and very expensive equipment, but you can produce temperatures part-way down the scale with little difficulty.

The range of temperatures on the two most common scales in public use start at 0 degrees centigrade and 32 degrees Fahrenheit. Both are the freezing point of water. The range downward is to absolute zero, which is −273C and −460F. At absolute zero all molecular motion theoretically ceases. Nothing could be colder.

Cryogenic temperatures are near this theoretical limit, for the temperature at which the gas helium becomes a liquid is only 46.5 Fahrenheit degrees above absolute zero, or 413.5 degrees below zero Fahrenheit.

At these temperatures materials develop a whole new set of characteristics. Some materials develop a kind of supersensitivity. Because there is so little molecular motion, there is little "noise" caused by such motion in the system itself. This has allowed the development of such devices as the cryotron and maser, both of which operate at cryogenic temperatures. The lack of internal "noise," (in the electronics sense, meaning unwanted effects) enabled scientists to receive radar signals bounced off the planet Venus in 1959 and off the sun itself in 1960.

Scientists have found that some metals become superconductors at low temperatures. The electrical resistance of materials is changed. There is even hope of a new source of energy, because the highly energetic, electrically unbalanced chemical particles called free radicals can be captured and frozen at cryogenic temperatures. Free radicals are very short lived at ordinary temperatures, and it took very low temperatures to capture them long enough for study. Much remains to be learned about them. It is known, however, that they release their energy after being frozen and rewarmed.

The experiment in which you can approach the strange world of cryogenics produces temperatures of −100F, or even slightly lower. Ordinary things change characteristics at these temperatures—and you can change abruptly, too, if you do not exercise care. You wouldn't like the change, so don't try. If possible, get father, older brother, or some interested adult to work with you.

You will need: an ovenproof glass bowl, or a pyrex laboratory beaker. Such glassware does not crack easily with temperature changes. You will also need heavy gloves, tongs of some kind, dry ice, and alcohol. You should also plan to work out of doors. Dry ice can be obtained from ice cream supply houses. Look up "dry ice" in the classified section of the telephone book. Ordinary alcohol can be used but 90% alcohol is best.

Chunks of dry ice are placed in the bowl; then alcohol is added. Don't overfill the bowl. Leave room for experiments. The alcohol will bubble and boil at first, and much vapor will be given off. This vapor is the reason for working outdoors. The winds will carry it away, and the heavy odor of alcohol with it. Alcohol vapor is flammable, so keep fire away.

When the alcohol has reached the temperature of the dry ice the boiling will cease. The dry ice will be softened. The temperature will be from −100F to −105F, depending on conditions.

If you can obtain liquid mercury, the mixture will freeze it solidly. You can even hammer a nail with it. Mercury freezes at −40F, a temperature found in some of our northern states in winter.

CRYOGENICS

Try immersing fruit in the dry ice-alcohol mixture. A banana, normally a soft and squashy fruit, becomes rock hard. Try to mash it with a hammer and it breaks into fragments. This is also dramatic when done with a hot dog.

What the mixture will do to fruit it will also do to fingers. If you were to make the mistake of putting your hand on the bowl, it would be necessary to leave large patches of skin behind to get it free. Wear the gloves at all times, and avoid touching either bowl or liquid; don't even touch the tong tips or experimental materials.

If your main interest is biology, obtain some natural cheese. Pasteurized cheese will not do, because you want live cheese bacteria in the samples. Sterilize two jars and caps by boiling. Put an untreated bit of cheese in one for a control, using sterilized tongs. Freeze another piece of cheese in the mixture and put it into the other jar, again with sterilized tongs. Observe the cheese and note any differences after several days. See if you can demonstrate that freezing does not kill cheese bacteria.

If you have cultured paramecia for your microscopy work, freeze some of the culture which you are sure has organisms in it, place in a sterile jar and re-culture to see if freezing has killed all organisms and spores.

If electronics and electricity are your interests, immerse the rheostat described on page 221 and check for variations in carbon resistance.

Your own imagination will produce other experiments, such as checking the effect of low temperatures on seed germination, or changed characteristics of fibrous materials like wood and cloth, and so on. And as you work, think about living in such temperatures. Men do, in the Antarctic.

EXPERIMENT IN COSMIC AND OTHER RADIATIONS

Have you ever seen a cosmic ray? You may have seen reproductions of cosmic-ray tracks on photographic emulsions, but it's unlikely that you've seen a cosmic-ray trail "in person," so to speak.

It's equally unlikely that you've seen other radiations. Those produced by natural radioactive elements are alpha, beta and gamma. Alpha rays are made up of alpha particles, which are like helium atoms with all electrons removed. That is, they consist of two each of the elementary nuclear particles called protons and neutrons. Beta rays are produced by the emission of beta particles, which are like electrons. (Or they may be like positrons, which have the same characteristics as electrons except for a positive instead of a negative charge.) Gamma rays are not particles, but pure energy. They are found in the electromagnetic spectrum along with radio waves, light and X rays. They fall just above X rays in the spectrum.

COSMIC RADIATION

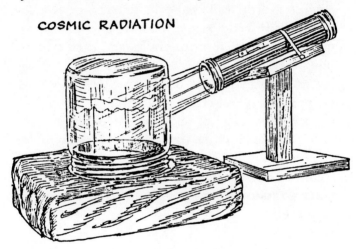

You can see some of these radiations, using dry ice and alcohol, in a device known as a Cloud Chamber. This is a standard tool used by physicists to observe particles and rays. Some very fancy cloud chambers have been made for precision work, but you can make a simple one quite easily.

You will need: A metal screw-top jar that is about as wide as it is high. One brand of peanut butter comes in such a jar. You will also need that old black felt cowboy hat from the junk box in the closet, or some other source of black felt. You may need some wire. If so, a coat hanger will do. Some old newspapers are easily obtained. So is a source of light in a narrow beam, like a movie or still picture projector, a flashlight, or the illuminator for your microscope.

Cut circles of felt to fit both bottom of the jar and jar cap. Remove the wax insert from the jar cap first. The fit should be very tight—as nearly perfect as you can make it. Circles can be inscribed with a compass, if you have one; or you can use the jar itself to draw circles and then trim to fit.

Cut a strip of felt one inch wide and long enough to make a circle just inside the mouth of the jar. This band of felt should touch the circle of felt in the jar cover when the top is screwed on.

The jar will be used upside down. If there seems to be any danger of the felt falling down, make a retaining ring of stiff wire to hold the felt in place.

Wrap a block of dry ice in newspaper to insulate it. Cut a hole large enough so the jar top will rest on the dry ice.

Soak the felts in alcohol. It is better to use too much than too little. Assemble the jar and put it metal-top down on the dry ice. Adjust your light so it shines downward into the jar, at an angle through the side.

A kind of alcohol mist will begin to precipitate almost at once. This will continue until the system has become stable, which will take about fifteen minutes.

Watch the jar from near the projector. When

all is stable, cosmic rays will appear as vapor trails in the jar. You will be able to see them against the black felt background. Cosmic rays are random. That is, they have no pattern of time or direction. You may get several in a moment, or just one now and then. Be patient, and keep your eyes open.

The temperature difference between the top of the cloud chamber and the icy metal at the bottom creates a dense alcohol vapor, in the same way that warmer air above cold earth can create fog. When a cosmic ray or other radiation passes through, it creates condensation nuclei on which the vapor can condense, producing a "line cloud" or vapor trail. This is not unlike the contrails produced by aircraft passing through an unstable part of the atmosphere.

Of course you do not actually see the ray or particle, which is submicroscopic and entirely invisible. You see its trail, or "cloudprint."

If you have a piece of uranium ore in your mineral collection, or if you can obtain one, put it near the jar. If there really is uranium in the specimen, you will see the tracks of gamma rays emitted by the radioactive mineral salt.

Hold a luminous watch dial close to the jar. You may see a few gamma rays, depending on the particular watch.

Gamma rays and cosmic rays will penetrate the glass jar. Alpha and beta particles will not.

If there is an old, discarded luminous dial watch around, ask for permission to ruin it permanently. Remove the dial and cut out a numeral. Use gloves and tinsmith's snips or a hacksaw. Use tweezers or needlenose pliers to handle the numeral. Wearing gloves, unscrew the jar cap, quickly insert the numeral, face up, and reassemble the jar. When the system re-stabilizes you should see a steady flow of tracks from the numeral. These are alpha and beta tracks produced by the radium in the luminous paint. This chamber will not work properly in humid air because of moisture condensation. Work in a dry place.

If your school has a radioactive source, you can put on a demonstration for your class. If it has a source, it also has a teacher who can help you. This teacher also will know about improved versions of cloud chambers, like expansion chambers, and a chamber made with a wide-mouth vacuum bottle, all of which can be made by the advanced experimenter.

EXPERIMENT IN STATIC ELECTRICITY

One of the earliest tools of the physicist in detecting radiations was the electroscope. Two very thin gold leaves were given an electrical charge. Since like charges repel, the leaves flew apart.

Radiation has the ability to ionize the air. That is, it tears electrons from atoms in the air, leaving them with an electrical charge. This is not too hard to understand if you think of an atom as a balanced electrical system. The central part, the nucleus, is electrically positive. Around this nucleus whirl electrons with negative charges, and there are just enough electrons to balance the positive charge of the nucleus.

Along comes a cosmic ray, a gamma ray, alpha or beta particles, or even a neutron. It strikes an atom a glancing blow and rips away one or more of the electrons.

The atom is now unbalanced. It has a positive charge. Electricity can flow among unbalanced atoms easily and rapidly, because the atoms try to regain electrical balance. The atoms can do this when new electrons are obtainable from somewhere else.

You can see what happens. Where the ray or particle passed, there is a line of unbalanced atoms of oxygen, nitrogen, carbon dioxide, or other elements of the air. So long as the air was composed of balanced atoms, it would not conduct electricity. Now, along the unbalanced line electrons flow from the charged leaves of the electroscope. With less charge, or no charge at all, the leaves do not repel each other and they fall together again.

Whether the leaves close all the way or only part way depends on the amount of ionization, which depends on the amount of radiation passing by.

You can make an electroscope of aluminum foil easily. One is shown in the illustration. The block on top of a clean jar is paraffin wax, which is a good insulator. But a plastic jar top or any other good insulator, including a waxed cork, also will do.

A piece of copper wire bent at the bottom to form a small shelf is thrust up through the paraffin or jar top. A strip of aluminum foil is draped over the wire.

To charge the electroscope, rub a comb with fur and let the charge from the comb run off into the copper wire. You might try charging the comb by rubbing the cat with it. Or you can use a piece of silk. The ends of the aluminum strip will move apart.

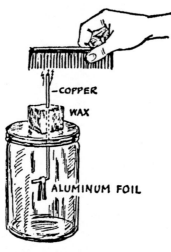

The electroscope will discharge eventually by itself, because air is not a perfect insulator (or dielectric, as it should be called in this case). Because of the water vapor in it, and because of cosmic rays and natural gamma radiation which are always present, air ordinarily conducts some electricity. See if you can hasten the discharge by putting the wristwatch numerals, or the uranium ore, in the jar.

You can also make an electroscope of two round balloons. Blow them up, tie them to two pieces of string, and tie the tops of the strings together so that the balloons hang together. Rub the balloons with silk. If there are no silk handkerchiefs in the house use one of dad's old silk ties. (It's better if he takes it off first.) Try other fabrics, too.

Since the charge on the two balloons will be the same, they will repel each other.

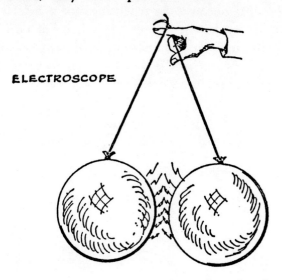

ELECTROSCOPE

The charge will leak off into the air after a while, but you can hasten the process with a source of radiation. However, the balloons will need much more radiation than the electroscope —more, probably, than you have available.

EXPERIMENT IN PERSISTENCE OF VISION

Among the things that depend on "persistence of vision"—the tendency of the eye to see the image for a brief time after the image has gone —is motion pictures.

Motion pictures consist of a series of still pictures of an action, taken at the rate of twenty-four pictures a second and projected at the same speed. When the series of pictures is projected, there is a brief interval between each picture when the screen is black, because a shutter flashes across the back of the lens as one picture is replaced by the next. Because we see things for a brief time after they are gone, we retain an image of a picture long enough for the next one to move into place. We do not notice the gap between pictures, and we see the series as continuous motion.

THAUMATROPE

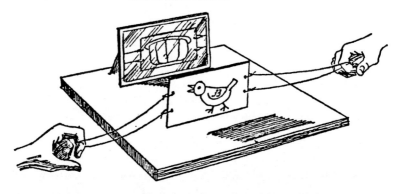

You can demonstrate persistence of vision with a simple gadget called a thaumatrope.

You will need: a piece of stiff card and some string.

On one side of the card draw a birdcage. On the other side draw a bird. Make it smaller than the cage. Attach the string as shown.

Hold the strings in both hands and have someone turn the card over and over, winding it up. When you pull on the strings they will unwind.

As the card spins rapidly the bird will appear in the cage.

EXPERIMENTS WITH ELECTRICITY AND ELECTROMAGNETISM

To make advanced electrical or electronic gadgets it is necessary to understand how electricity is produced and how it flows. As part of this understanding depends on knowing the properties of magnets. In these experiments it is assumed that you already know what a magnet is, that magnets have positive and negative poles, and that compass needles are magnets.

A COMPASS GALVANOMETER

You will need: a coil of bell wire, an inexpensive compass such as you buy in a toy store, and plastic tape. Your power source should be an electric lantern battery, which can be purchased at any hardware store.

Unwrap a few feet of wire from each end of the coil without unwrapping the entire coil. Tape the coil together in a few places. Scrape insulation from the ends of the wire to make connections.

Stand the coil upright on a piece of wood and tape it in place. Flatten out the bottom of the coil so the compass can rest steadily, and put the compass in place.

Turn coil and compass so that the compass points north and south and the coil direction is also north and south.

Connect one lead wire to the battery. Watch

the compass as you touch the other wire to the battery terminal.

The compass needle, being a magnet, has a magnetic field. The coil has none until current passes through it. Then the coil's field affects the needle's field and the result is a definite swing of the needle. As you experiment, find out whether changing the leads to the battery changes the di-

COMPASS GALVANOMETER

rection of swing, whether the needle always swings the same amount, and whether the swing is greater when you make contact or after the needle has had a chance to steady down.

The coil is an inductance. See if its properties change with less turns of wire.

A CARBON RHEOSTAT

A rheostat is a device that varies the amount of current in a circuit by changing the amount of resistance to the current flow. In experimenting with your galvanometer you can make a rheostat quite simply, connecting it between the positive terminal of the battery and one side of the coil.

You will need: a pair of spring clips and a very thick pencil lead. Pencils with leads about an eighth of an inch in diameter are sold, and there are also pencils that are made entirely of graphite with only a coating of thick paint. The carbon rod from the center of an old battery would be even better.

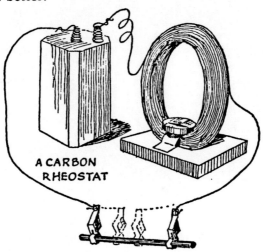

A CARBON
RHEOSTAT

The wire from the coil is attached to one clip, and the wire from the positive battery terminal to the other. The clips are then attached to the lead. (Remember, pencil lead is not metallic lead, but graphite, a form of carbon.)

The farther apart on the lead you place the clips, the more carbon there will be in the circuit. To lessen the amount of carbon—and the resistance—move the clips closer together. Check the compass needle each time to determine the amount of swing.

A MORE SENSITIVE GALVANOMETER

You can use the same coil, battery and rheostat to make a more powerful galvanometer. In addition, *you will need:* a sewing needle, large enough to handle comfortably; a few feet of enameled magnet wire like that used to wind the coil for the crystal radio; a bit of thread; and a strip of thin cardboard.

A MORE SENSITIVE GALVANOMETER

To magnetize the needle, wrap it from end to end with enameled wire, making turns as tight as you can. Then connect the ends of the wires to your battery. After a few minutes disconnect the wire from the battery and try to pick up iron filings or tacks with the needle. If the needle needs more magnetism, reconnect and give it more time.

Remove the coil of wire and attach the needle to a length of thread in such a way that it balances when you hold the thread. Make a slip knot in the thread and find the balance point by moving the needle in and out a bit at a time.

If you wipe the needle with alcohol before putting on the thread a bit of wax or glue will hold the knot in place, If you have trouble, lay the needle in a fold of plastic tape and run the thread through the tape.

Cut the cardboard so that it can be bent in a circle that just fits inside the coil. Remove the compass from the galvanometer. Put the thread through the center of the cardboard strip and secure it by knotting or wrapping around the strip. Bend the strip into place so that the needle hangs in the middle of the coil. You can adjust the thread properly by experimenting.

If you want to make accurate measurements, tape a strip of heavy white paper across the coil opening right below the needle. You can mark on the paper with a soft pencil. Turn the coil so the needle projects outward from the opening, and mark its normal position as zero on the paper strip. Start experimenting.

A VOLTAIC SALT CELL

In Chapter VII simple batteries to operate a transistor were described. Try them on the sensitive galvanometer and see if any results are obtained. Then make the more conventional cell first discovered by Volta, the Italian scientist who first learned to produce electricity by chemical action.

You will need: a water glass, salt, a strip of zinc cut from the outside of a used battery, and a strip of copper. Hobby shops or firms that deal in copper house gutters have copper scraps.

Make a saturated salt solution in the water glass. A saturated solution is one in which the solvent—water in this case—can hold no more material. Warm water will dissolve more salt than cold, so use it. Use muscle, too, to keep stirring until no more salt will dissolve.

VOLTAIC SALT CELL

Cut thin slits in one end of the zinc and copper strips. Force wires into the slits; then bend these ends over so that they will hang on the rim of the glass. Place the strips, wires hanging outside, on opposite sides of the rim.

Voltage will be registered on your galvanometer.

The action of the salt will soon cause a loss of efficiency. Restore the cell by wiping the strips. Wipe the copper strip more often, because it corrodes faster.

A similar battery can be made by substituting

dilute sulphuric acid for the salt solution. Bubbles will collect, causing a drop in current; but they can be shaken off. Acid is dangerous to handle. Even in dilute form it can ruin clothes. So get permission first.

A series of Voltaic cells can be made. If connected in series, the total voltage will equal the combined voltage of the cells. If connected in parallel, the voltage will remain the same, but there

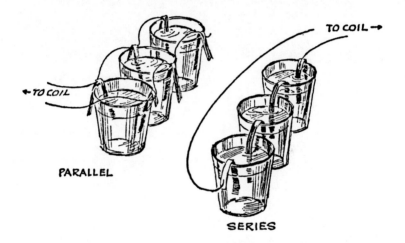

will be more current. The difference between a series and a parallel circuit is shown in the illustration.

AN ELECTROMAGNET

The bell wire from the galvanometer coil can be used to make an electromagnet. **You will need:** a two-inch machine bolt with two washers, obtainable at any hardware store.

Put the washers on the bolt, then screw the nut

on until the end of the bolt just reaches the top of the hole. Separate the washers and wind wire onto the bolt. Neatness helps. Leave a few feet of wire loose when you start, and as much more when you finish winding. Tape will hold the coil in place.

When connected to your lantern battery, the bolt becomes an electromagnet. Try it out. When

ELECTROMAGNET

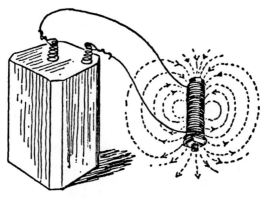

you have a load of iron on the bolt, disconnect and see how much of the load the bolt retains.

The coil and current will induce magnetism in the bolt, so magnetism will remain even after the battery is disconnected. However, there will be less power. Try leaving the current connected for different lengths of time and observe the effect on the bolt's magnetic strength.

You can combine Rick's interests with Scotty's and make a game with the bolt electromagnet. Let the magnet dangle by its wires from an old fishing pole or a pole cut from a broomstick. This will form a fishing pole, line and magnetic bait.

Fish can be anything the magnet will pick up. Assorted nails can be fished for in a bucket or cardboard carton. Washers can be used, with pictures, numbers or names pasted on them. Fishing for partners is a good ice-breaker for a party.

EXPERIMENT IN PHOTOGRAPHY

A pinhole camera is a light-proof box with film at one end and a pinhole in the other. When the pinhole is opened, by removing a bit of opaque tape, the film is exposed. If there is enough light, a picture is taken.

You can make a pinhole camera from a shoebox without much trouble, but it will be necessary to use cut film and to load the camera in a dark room. It really isn't worth the trouble, even though Rick had to try it just to prove that it worked.

The problem was, he didn't prove it to Barby. She insisted he had taken the pictures with a hidden camera, not with the shoebox.

In desperation, Rick finally made a giant pinhole camera that convinced her.

To duplicate the experiment, **you will need:** black construction paper, several feet of white wrapping paper of the kind used by some drugstores, tape, scissors, and an assortment of needles and nails of various sizes. You will also need a large cardboard carton, one big enough for you to fit into comfortably. Appliance and department stores are good sources, because TV consoles, refrigerators, washing machines and other large appliances come in such cartons. Get one with a top if you can, because it must be made lightproof.

Put the box in strong sunlight, get inside and
have someone close you in. You can see where
light leaks in and direct the placing of heavy tape,
thin cardboard taped in place or other means of
sealing out the light. The entrance to the box can
be sealed with a thick blanket.

When the box is at last light-proof, decide
which end will be the "film" and which will contain the pinhole. Cover the "film" end with white
paper.

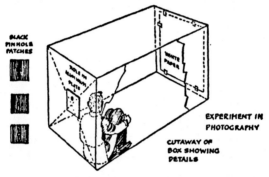

Find the center of the pinhole end by drawing
lines from opposite corners. Where the lines cross
is the center. Two inches above the center make a
hole the size of a quarter. Cut it out with a knife;
it need not be smooth and perfect.

Cut the black paper into squares that will cover
the hole with room to spare, to allow for taping.
Make a number of pinholes of varying size, one
to a square. Start with the needles and end with
a tenpenny nail.

If you find it hard to make a clean hole by pok-
ing the needle or nail through, a clean hole can
be burned through with a red hot needle or nail.

If you try this, get permission. A mother who sees her needles heating is apt to heat up under the collar. She may even be tempted to conduct an experiment in heating by percussion, on a tender part of your anatomy.

You are ready when the pinholes are. Be sure that the pinhole side of the box faces the sun. One refinement is advisable. If you have a sheet of scrap aluminum, cut a quarter-size hole and tape the metal to the cardboard so that the holes match up. This is because a tape-to-metal contact releases smoothly, but a tape-to-cardboard contact tears the cardboard and messes up the tape.

Place a fellow experimenter in the box and seal out light. He won't smother during the few minutes he will be inside. Put a pinhole in place and cover it.

The inside man will need from three to five minutes for his eyes to adapt to the darkness. It helps if his eyes are covered for a few minutes before he gets into the box.

After three minutes uncover the pinhole and walk about fifteen feet away. If there is enough light the inside man will see you, in full color, projected upside down on the white paper "film." If he has a small sheet of white paper, notebook size, he can hold it in front of the pinhole and experiment with focus.

Remember that lots of sunlight is needed, and the object to be viewed should be fully illuminated.

As in all cameras, the better the light and the smaller the hole, the clearer and sharper the picture. Experiment with pinholes of different sizes to see which works the best.

Barby was convinced when she viewed the experiment from inside the box. At first Rick had trouble persuading her to keep her head out of the way of the pinhole, but once she crouched out of the line of light, she became a convert to the simplest form of photography.

EXPERIMENTS AND READING

Library shelves seem to be crowded with books on scientific experiments. You can find just about anything from experiments with soap to building a full-scale transmitter. Your librarian is there to help. Consult her, and learn how to use the card index. You'll find many books that will interest you.

It's important to do some reading while experimenting. Otherwise you can't get the most out of your equipment. Don't be like the little boy who thought he had to draw his own pictures on the TV tube with crayon because he didn't know how to plug the set in.

A real scientist is never satisfied until he has explored all possible avenues with his equipment. If something strange happens, he tries to find out why. Sometimes he comes across a whole new and wonderful world. Fleming, in England, was doing some routine work when a little mold blew in a window and contaminated one of his cultures— and, because he was a scientist, he investigated the strange behavior of the culture and found penicillin. For that matter, Columbus was searching for a passage to India—and look what he found. Scientists have a word for this kind of event, and you can experiment in philology in an unabridged dictionary by looking it up. The word is:

SERENDIPITY

Chapter X

About Science Projects

Rick promptly put it [his new microscope] to work on a science project in which he planned to compare the life cycles of two common microscopic animals. . . .

from THE BLUE GHOST MYSTERY
Chapter I, *A Spooky Invitation.*

SCIENCE PROJECTS are such a fast-growing part of school life that few students can escape them. There are thousands of science clubs, and more science is being taught in many schools. In addition to the National Science Fair, there are local science fairs, some under school sponsorship, some under non-school clubs.

If you are interested in science, you are very likely to end up with a science project once or several times in your school life. The purpose of this chapter is to describe some of the things Rick Brant, other science projecteers, and professional scientists have learned about how to conduct and show a project.

Science projects can be real fun or sheer horror. It depends on the spirit in which you get started, including why you got started in the first place. The only real reason for doing a science project is to *want* to do one.

Wrong approach: "I can't play ball today, Joe. We're having a science fair and I've got to whomp up some kind of project. Wish I knew what I could do that's easy."

Right approach: "I asked the teacher if that plastic spray you buy in a can would keep my bike spokes from rusting. He told me to find out for myself and let him know. Well, I got so interested I'm making a science project out of it. It's called, 'Effectiveness of common protective films in preventing oxidation of metals.'"

But let's say you have a science project you want to do. The first question is: What is a science project?

Simply, it's an investigation. It describes something and tries to find out what it is, what caused it, what changes it, what can be made to happen to it, whether it's useful or damaging, or anything else that will explain it.

A science project is not gadgetry for its own sake. True, national prizes have been won by science projects built on the construction of something unusual. But, equally true, national prizes have been won by studies that produced nothing but a report and a few simple charts.

The second question is: How do you choose a science study?

The answer is: If you have an inquiring mind, science projects will choose you. Anything you wonder about in nature or some aspects of human life can be the basis for a science study.

If this seems too general to be helpful, consider some examples.

1. You notice that an outdoor light left on at night attracts bugs by the hundreds. You wonder why. Nearly everyone wonders about this at some time or another, but it's amazing how few try to find out. You try, and you find that some of life's creatures have a characteristic called phototropism. You knew that, of course, from watching the bugs, but now you have a name for it.

You realize that you are not equipped to look into the bug's physiology to study the electrochemical action that causes this, but you're curious. What kind of light attracts what kind of insect? Does color make a difference? Does intensity? Does light size? How about distance?

Here's a science project in the making. You can answer these questions by experimentation. Your parents will doubtless be very tired of bugs by the time you're through, but you can find some answers. Your experimental setup will be the basis for an exhibit. Your notes and tables will be the basis for a report.

2. Your team plays another school team, and in listening to all the talk you notice that most everyone from the other school hails everyone as "Hey, Sam!"

This is ridiculous, because they can't all be named Sam, especially the girls. Your school is much more sensible. You all hail friends with a "Hey, Skip." This way, no one is confused, because no one is named Skip, but all either skip school or don't skip school, so the name fits.

A science project in this? Yes, and an unusual

one. If you get curious about the differences in common chatter between students in different schools, or even in different grades within the same school, you have opened up a whole series of questions.

Between schools there are often many differences. Entirely different terms may be used for the unhappy lot of a student who must spend all free time in the principal's office, for example. Or there may be different meanings for a single word.

Compare terms and definitions. Try to track down the origins of the phrases. Estimate what percentage of students in each school use the phrases. See if students in the different schools come from generally different kinds of homes. For instance, in school X, because of its location, are most of the students from families that work in the local industry? Are school Y families mostly drawn from professionals? How about differences in national origins. Do school X families generally come from an area largely populated by Swedes, Poles, Italians, Germans, or some other national group?

Comparison is best done on charts that provide a basis for an exhibit. Your methods, details of data, and any conclusions will form the report. A good project of this kind would rate you the title of Cultural Anthropologist, Novice Class.

3. Ever build a soap-box car? If so, you probably had trouble making a decent brake. Of course you might not have bothered, wearing out shoe leather instead by foot-dragging. But if you made an effec-

tive brake, it could be the basis for a science project on "Designs for Friction Brakes in Soap-Box Cars Using Common Materials."

Braking is a problem in engineering. Leverage is a primary part. So are the properties of common materials, including hard and soft woods and scrap metals. Much could be said about rope versus wire. Methods of obtaining what is called "mechanical advantage" would need to be explored.

Engineering projects are just as important as science projects, and an investigation into braking could give you a reputation as a budding mechanical engineer.

These are examples of the wide range possible in science projects. You may get ideas from your reading, from questions that arise in science class, or from trying to help solve a problem at home— such as why all the house plants died at the same time.

National Science Fairs are sponsored by Science Service, Inc., which has published a small pamphlet called *Thousands of Science Projects*. There are many pages of projects that actually have been conducted, all classified by subject. A copy can be obtained for 25¢ from Science Clubs of America, 1719 N.St., N.W., Washington 6, D. C.

The range of projects is interesting. Just about all fields of science are covered, and the kind of project runs from an analysis of the egg and bottle experiment (a very old trick way of getting an egg into a milk bottle) to Experimental Determination of Acetylcholine in the Human Spinal Fluid. (This chemical, which is produced by our bodies, plays a vital role in such "automatic" actions as breathing.)

So, the universe sets the limits on science projects, insofar as the subjects are concerned. Actual selection of a project, however, depends on some practical limitations.

The first limitation is your own ability, and the second is time. They go together. As with everything else, you learn how to do a science project by actually doing. For your first project, choose something simple, something well within your abilities. You can undertake the more complicated projects later on.

Figure out how much time you have. Don't toss off a figure like "three months." It doesn't mean anything. How much time will you actually have to work on a science project? Be realistic. Then compare the time with your own ability.

It has happened far too often that a science projecteer has taken on more than he could handle and been forced to work through the night, with his haggard parents helping in order to finish on time. Don't get yourself into a jam like that. It's no fun, and a science project that isn't fun is pretty deadly. It's apt not to be a very good job, either.

There are other limitations, too. Money is one. Excellent projects can be conducted at very low cost, but few can be conducted for nothing. At the very least you will need poster paint, artist's board and other supplies for making your display. Count your costs in advance.

For every project there are some practical limitations. You may be wild about snakes, while your mother and sister fall over in a dead faint at the sight of one. It's practical to forget your passion for reptiles and drop herpetology as a project.

Once you have taken all factors into account and decided on a project, it is time to make A PLAN.

Any scientist will tell you that an experiment is performed on paper before it goes to the lab, and those that aren't turn out to be pretty sad. A properly prepared plan tells you what you're going to do and how you're going to do it. A plan is the blueprint of the project. Like the blueprint of a house, it tells you the size and shape of the project, what it will look like, the door by which you will enter, the door by which you will leave, and the rooms you will cross enroute.

Start your plan by writing a statement of your objectives. "This project will attempt to find out if the blinking of fireflies has a definite pattern, and even if some kind of regular 'language' is involved. The project will consider temperature, humidity, variations according to the amount of darkness, any differences between wooded and open areas, and variations due to the number of fireflies in a given area."

See if you can, at this point, give the project an accurate title. The title should tell anyone looking at it the general subject of the project.

Describe the method. In order to avoid introducing artificial factors, you will observe the firefly in his native habitat. This means you will obtain some method of counting firefly flashes, perhaps by borrowing a hand counter. You will also mark out three areas of the same size. One will be woods, the other open field, the third a mixture, perhaps with low shrubs.

Once the method is described in great detail, take another look at the objectives and title. What will the method give you? It may produce a machine, seeds germinated under a variety of conditions, or—in the case of the fireflies—a series of numbers.

Where series of numbers are concerned, the best form of presentation is tables, with the tables simplified as much as possible for easy reading by observers at the science fair, who are usually in a hurry.

Does this modify your title? In the firefly project, for instance, it might show you that "A Statistical Approach to Visual Firefly Communication" would be most descriptive.

Now put down the form your conclusions will take. This is a key to how your project will be presented. Of course you won't know the conclusions in advance—at least in definite form. But you may have enough data to put them down in a rough outline.

Recheck your blueprint. Think about it. Revise it. Keep revising it as you learn more about what you're doing.

Think about illustrating the experiment. Can

you use actual apparatus to show the method?
How about photographs? Specimens? Jot down the
plan for exhibiting your project.

Now, with your plans outlined, stop and think
about troubles you might get into, especially the
possibility that something may go wrong and leave
you with no time for doing the experiment over.
Go over every step in your own mind.

At this point, your blueprint—no matter how
hard you've worked on it—should be marked
"Preliminary and Tentative."

Start reading. Your librarian will help you;
your science teacher can suggest books. If there is
a college or university near you, consult its library. If there is a laboratory nearby with a general field of operations that matches yours, call
whomever is in charge of education or public re-
lations and arrange to ask questions of experts.

Scientists do not work alone. Even the single
individual at his lonely bench is not alone and un-
aided. The world of science is with him, through
the reports of other scientists in his field. Every
scientist depends on the work of others. Einstein
developed his special and general theories by
drawing on the works of Planck, Fitzgerald, Lo-
rentz, and many others. What's more, he gave
them full credit.

You are not only allowed to draw on the works
of others, you are not working properly unless
you do. Look at any issue of *Science,* the weekly
publication of the American Association for the
Advancement of Science. Examine the reports,

and note that very, very few are without a list of papers at the end. These papers are the acknowledgment of the authors that they drew on the works of others.

Skimming through the indexes of a few issues, by the way, is a very good method of seeing for yourself that the world of science is very wide and very deep.

A caution, however. Do not impose on the good nature of adults without reason. Don't ask them to do something you could do yourself—like looking in the library's card catalogue. Don't pay a visit to a biologist who specializes in fireflies until you have studied enough to be able to ask intelligent questions.

When you've studied, questioned, planned and replanned, talk over the whole project with someone. Your science teacher or advisor would be a good one; so would an intelligent classmate with some experience in science projects.

Your parents may be helpful, depending on their background.

Talking it over helps clarify the project in your own mind, and it gives someone else a fresh look that may show some holes you hadn't thought of.

Now you're about ready to begin. Get a notebook and start keeping detailed notes. You may think this is a nuisance, but do it anyway. Be faithful to your notebook and it will repay you a thousandfold. Record everything, including failures. Thomas Edison's notebooks are full of failures—but then, the great inventor knew that it's as important to know something doesn't work as to know that something does. It saves trying it again later on.

Do your work with care, and try to perfect your technique. If it's a biology experiment that requires sterile technique, never fail to flame the mouth of the test tube. Follow procedure as carefully as you can, until perfection is simply a way of working.

Keep in mind at all times, though, that you are not an adult scientist. You may be one someday, but right now you're a junior. No one expects the kind of deep analysis, complicated mathematical proofs, or elegant, original experiments of the professional. But everyone does expect a neat, thoughtful and complete job of work.

While the experiment is still in progress, but when you've reached a point where some data has been compiled, start your report. Put down the objectives in readable form, as briefly as completeness allows. Describe the method, also as briefly as you can.

Results follow, with conclusions last, unless recommendations are called for.

The best English is simple English. Short sentences are better than long ones. Simple words are better than unusual ones.

Project titles given throughout this book are pretty elaborate, and are by way of being a joke —a caricature of real titles of scientific papers. The joke is only partial, however. Scientists overdo it, sometimes, but the main reason for the rather cumbersome titles is that scientists always try to be precise. They try to title their papers so that other scientists can see at once what the subject matter contains.

For the same reason, scientists include a summary, which is called an "abstract," at the start of the paper. This is a good approach for a science project report, too. It may even be required for some fairs, and is a definite requirement for others. A summary should contain a brief statement of the objectives, an indication of the method without going into details, and a brief statement of the main conclusions.

Scientists go in for fancy language now and then, but you should avoid it. Scientists should, too; and when they fail to write simply, they may find someone having a laugh at their expense. Sometimes, scientific and technical journals will carry funny articles about how not to write scientific reports, using language that many report writers use.

One example was a short course for research report writers that was carried in *Metal Progress*, a technical magazine. The article was a list of phrases used over and over again in reports, with an explanation in *italics* of what each phrase really means. These are samples:

"It has long been known that . . ." *I haven't bothered to look up the original reference.*

". . . of great theoretical and practical importance . . ." *interesting to me.*

". . . accidently strained during mounting . . ." *dropped on the floor.*

". . . handled with extreme care during the experiment . . ." *not dropped on the floor.*

"It is clear that much additional work will be required before a complete understanding has been achieved . . ." *I don't understand it.*

"Unfortunately, a quantitative theory to account for these effects has not been formulated . . ." *nobody else understands it, either.*

The real meaning of these amusing samples, slightly changed from the original article to make the meanings clearer to junior scientists, is that no one is really fooled by fancy phrases. Only the real merit of the project impresses anyone, and clear, simple English will help to show the project to best advantage.

As you advance in your science projects, more help will be needed. Fortunately, more help is available if you know where to look for it, and if you know what to ask for. The kind of help that will do your science project for you is not common, so know what you need when you look for help.

The most common kind of letter received by societies, companies or institutions is the one that goes, "please send me (free) everything you have on Prodsponders." The person receiving the letter gives a sorrowful sigh, sticks a couple of standard pamphlets in an envelope, adds a form letter, and mails it off. After all, "everything you have" on Prodsponders amounts to ninety-seven tons of technical reports, a full library housed in a separate building, and several thousand bits of information stored on tape in the memory banks of a digital computer.

The outfit does, however, have a number of reports, leaflets and pamphlets on different aspects of Prodsponders, which they will send to anyone intelligent enough to let them know his exact interests.

In contrast, the letter may read, "In developing a science project with the purpose of finding out how Prodsponders wheep, I built a whimpling chamber with an inside dimension of ten cubic inches. By adding 2 cc. of landersprang juice, I got the Prodsponder sample to wheep once, but most of the time the wheep is only partial, generally resembling a whop more than a wheep. I have rechecked my experimental setup in accordance with Dvual's article in the September issue of the *Prodsponder Monthly*, with no success. My supplier assures me that the Prodsponder sample is accurate, and I have run the juice through an ion exchange column to insure purity. Can you advise me on any elements I may have overlooked? Your help will be sincerely appreciated."

The answer goes back at once. ". . . so your difficulty is almost certainly in impurities in the landersprang juice which cannot be extracted by ion exchange. We suggest you obtain a quantity from our own supplier, Rameses Landersprangs, Inc. This company guarantees purity. Please let us know if this better grade of juice causes the Prodsponder to wheep, and by all means let us see a copy of your report."

But you get the idea.

A specific question will bring a specific answer —unless the answer can be found in any convenient reference and you were too lazy to look it up. A famous radio question-and-answer man, noted for being able to answer anything, once did a kind of science project on his own mail and reported that answers to over ninety percent of the questions he was asked could have been found in the dictionary, almanac or encyclopedia—if the listener had bothered to look them up.

Where do you get this kind of expert help? If you have read enough to need such assistance, you will know the answer from your reading. You will know what scientific societies there are in the field, what companies manufacture the materials on which your project is centered, and so on. Your own local advisors will also know where to get help that they cannot provide.

For general information on science projects, The Future Scientists of America Foundation of the National Science Teacher's Association, 1201 16th St., N.W., Washington 6, D. C., has a booklet for 50 cents called *If You Want to Do a Science Project*.

If you've had no experience at all in experimenting, a good way to begin is to arrange for your folks to give you a birthday subscription to *Things of Science,* a monthly experimental package issued by Science Service, Inc. Each month brings a little blue box or envelope containing materials and instructions for science experiments. The kits are self-contained. There is nothing additional to buy.

Few things are more fun than a science project, if you plan it well and have enough time so that you can complete it without being "pushed." Try it and see. On the other hand, don't underrate your capabilities. You can do more than you think you can. As the old jingle says:

"*Bite off more than you can chew,*
    And chew it.
Think of more than you can do,
    And do it.
Hitch your wagon to a star,
Keep your seat and there you are.
    Go to it.

Printed in the United States
53045LVS00001B/21

9 781557 090089